Just when Doña Maria... is over and Napoleon's... captured by French off... to hold her hostage so... by her lover, the infamous guerrilla leader Felipe Marquez, will attempt to rescue her. It *should* be easy for Mariana to hate Dupré, whose compatriots have already killed her brother and now threaten the man to whom she is pledged. Instead, she finds herself unwillingly drawn to her captor . . .

It seems that if she is to find happiness Mariana must turn traitor, but which will she betray—her country or her heart?

DAUGHTER OF SPAIN

ANN HULME

MILLS & BOON LIMITED
London · Sydney · Toronto

*First published in Great Britain 1984
by Mills & Boon Limited, 15–16 Brook's Mews,
London W1A 1DR*

© Ann Hulme 1984
*Australian copyright 1984
Philippine copyright 1984*

ISBN 0 263 74728 X

Set in 11 on 12½ pt Linotron Times
04–0784–53,000

*Photoset by Rowland Phototypesetting Ltd
Bury St Edmunds, Suffolk
Made and printed in Great Britain by
Cox & Wyman Ltd, Reading*

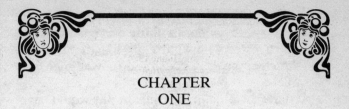

CHAPTER
ONE

'TAKE CARE! If you build that fire so high, it will be seen down in the valley!'

Despite this hoarse shout of protest, one of the men threw an armful of brushwood on to the crackling flames, sending them leaping wildly even higher into the blue-black sky, shooting out great twisting tongues of orange, yellow and red.

'Colours like the Spanish flag, eh, señorita?' the man beside Mariana chuckled.

The slim young girl to whom he spoke pulled her shawl further over her head, peasant fashion, and urged, 'Go and tell Don Felipe I'm here, José. Where is he?'

José vanished into the surrounding blackness, away from the magic circle of dancing light, and Mariana shrank back too.

It was growing late in the year. The barren hillsides, which had been scorched brown by the summer sun, now showed the first signs of approaching winter. On their exposed slopes, the winds blew sharply across from the distant High Pyrenees, and the nights were chill. On a clear day, the majestic peaks of the great range, a natural barrier between Spain and France, could be seen

from this vantage-point, grey-green in a dusky
haze. In another month those distant summits
would be frosted with white caps, like sugar cakes,
and the steep goat-tracks would be well-nigh im-
passable.

Mariana shivered in the chill air. She would have
liked to move closer to the warmth of the flames,
but hesitated to do so. It was not the danger of
flying sparks she feared, but the wild coarse faces of
the men around the fire. Though they knew who
she was, and would not harm her, yet there was a
primitive savagery in those unshaven faces beneath
the stocking caps which made Mariana pull the
edges of the shawl about her face and seek the
sanctuary of the shadows beyond the firelight.

These *guerrilleros* had been hiding in the hills
and fighting the French since 1808, and now, in late
1813, they sensed that, at last, the French were on
the run. One after another, the northern strong-
holds had succumbed to the British. King Joseph
Bonaparte had abandoned the Spanish crown
given to him by his brother, Napoleon, and had
fled.

All over Spain, bands of Spanish guerrilla
fighters like those men about the fire were coming
down from the hills, bloodstained and victorious.
Perhaps that was why they built the fire so high.
Scenting victory, they were growing bold, even
careless.

The fire spat and crackled and, attracted by the
noise and the showers of golden sparks which
rained down in an impromptu firework display,

Mariana failed to notice the figure of a man who had approached her softly through the darkness, until a hand touched her arm.

'Why are you standing out here?' asked a concerned voice. 'José is a fool. He should have brought you straight to me.'

Mariana jumped, her heart leaping into her mouth, then gave a sigh of relief. 'Oh, Felipe, I brought—'

'Wait, wait,' he interrupted. 'Come with me.'

He took her arm to guide her as she stumbled beside him over the uneven ground. Suddenly a ramshackle shelter of branches loomed up, a blanket draped across the 'doorway'. This was thrown aside, and Mariana ducked her head and entered.

'Welcome to my house!' Felipe said courteously. 'It is yours.'

It might have been a palace, from the tone of his voice.

A stub of tallow candle burned on an improvised table. Mariana pushed back the shawl from her chestnut hair, and turned to face the guerrilla leader. His head of long, unkempt, black hair brushed the roof of his primitive abode, and the light of the candle flickered across his lean, sunburned face, emphasising the hollows about the dark eyes and the aquiline nose. Felipe Marquez, nicknamed 'the White Wolf', on whose head the French had set a price which was almost a king's ransom, and at whose name the peasants in the valley below, made the sign of the Cross, often following this by spitting through their fingers to ward away the Evil Eye.

He stood quite still, watching her almost broodingly, and, conscious of the tiny, confined space, Mariana drew back a little.

Unexpectedly, he took her hand and bowed over it elegantly. Mariana felt a nervous desire to laugh aloud. She would not have dared. Yet the irony was that, even here, even in such circumstances, unshaven and dirty, Felipe was a Spanish *hidalgo* still. No matter that he wore the same rough clothes as the men he led, even the soft rope-soled sandals laced by leather thongs, which enabled a man to move silently over the rocks. No matter the brutal reputation and the fearsome legend. The most casual observer would have seen at once that this was no hill shepherd or illiterate brigand, this was a Spanish nobleman, however strangely disguised.

Perhaps he guessed what was in her mind, because he smiled and shrugged.

'It will only be for a little longer,' he said, adding a trifle ruefully, 'I am in need of a bath, and now that the day grows near when I shall be able again to live like a decent human being, I confess I dream of such luxury!'

'I brought the razor you asked for, and the soap,' Mariana said. 'Also a roast chicken.'

He chuckled. 'You are an angel. Even after such a long time in the hills, I find I cannot live like a peasant, on gazpacho.' His tone sharpened. 'What news of Wellington?'

'Everyone says the British will push on into

France,' Mariana told him, her voice expressing some doubt. 'Some say it will be any day, others that it will take longer.' She sighed. 'The French stand and fight, fall back, stand again. All the time they are driven back. But never without a fight. It could be months.'

Felipe snapped his fingers carelessly. 'No matter. What are a few months after five years? They are beaten. "Tio Pepe" has run back to brother Napoleon,' he went on, referring to the luckless King Joseph by the derisive nickname, signifying 'Uncle Joe', that the Spanish had given him. 'The French army must follow him. Those who linger, will do so for ever—in a Spanish grave! As for the miserable *afrancesados* who betrayed their Spanish blood to take service under him—they have run away too, like the rats they are!'

'But the French are still here!' Mariana said urgently. 'I came to tell you, Felipe, to warn you, not to send down to the village.'

'The French are in the village?' he demanded sharply. 'Wait, sit down.'

He indicated a chunk of upturned tree-trunk which served as a stool, and, as she sat down, he rummaged in the back of his hut and produced a grimy bottle and two chipped glasses.

From outside, by the fire, came the sound of someone plucking at a guitar. It was a pretty, sentimental tune, punctuated in gipsy fashion by abrupt changes of rhythm, marked by strummed chords and a rapid tapping on the wood. Perhaps the guitarist was impatient, too, to quit the hills and rejoin his buxom sloe-eyed Rosita or Conchita in the whitewashed village below.

'We shall drink a glass of the best wine my cellar can offer you!' Felipe said, not without humour, as he poured it out with a flourish. 'And then you can tell me everything.'

Mariana did not want the wine, but feared to insult his *hidalgo* pride by refusing his hospitality. She sipped at it cautiously. It was a rough, local vintage, of an almost purplish red. It left a sour taste in her mouth and furred her teeth.

'You know the great country house belonging to the Duchess,' she asked, setting down the glass, half full, 'on the Madrid highroad?'

'Of course I know it!' He smiled at her. 'I went to a ball there once. Have you forgotten? I shall never forget. Miguel had promised to present me to his little sister—and he presented me to the most beautiful girl in all Spain.'

He put his hand over hers and Mariana looked down, away from the ardent admiration expressed in his eyes.

Yes, she remembered. She had been only fifteen, and fresh from convent school. She had dreamed about the ball for weeks beforehand. She had been dazed by the magnificence of the great house, the huge oil portraits in the entrance hall, the great gilded ballroom, the multi-coloured tapestries, the sparkling crystal of the chandeliers, the heat and glow of thousands of candles, and the lilting music. Startled, she had found herself surrounded by handsome, dark-eyed young men, all expressing their devotion and showering extravagant compliments upon her. Among them had been Felipe, to whom she had paid especial heed because, her beloved brother Miguel had said, Felipe was a friend of his.

Five years ago. How much had happened since then, to Spain, to them all.

'I feel as though I have lived a whole lifetime since that night,' she said quietly. 'Will those days ever come back? Perhaps they can't.'

There was a way in which those days could never return, and they both knew it. So many of those handsome, bold, young men on whom the candlelight had shimmered that night now lay dead. Those whom French bullets and cannon had not claimed had fallen victim to the diseases which haunt armies. Hunger and extremes of heat and cold had weakened them. Gangrene, cholera, dysentery and typhus had finished the work.

'Miguel is dead,' Felipe said softly, knowing what was in her mind. 'I cannot bring him back to life, to you. But he has been avenged, that I swear. And when all this is over, we shall be married—and we shall make those days return.'

Mariana involuntarily pulled her hand from his. 'I . . . I cannot speak of that now, Felipe. Please. When it is all over, then we can talk about us.'

'I understand,' he said with some reluctance. 'Though I am not a man who finds it easy to be patient.' The candlelight threw its yellow glare over his features as he leaned towards her, and with his face so close to hers, she was afraid he would read the alarm in her eyes. She fixed her gaze on the table, trusting he would put her demeanour down to modesty.

'I think only of you,' Felipe whispered. 'The thought of you tortures me. To know you are so near—and yet so far from me is perpetual torment, as if I carried in my heart some throbbing wound which will not heal, unless at your touch . . .'

He fell silent, and Mariana, who had held her breath during his speech, drew a deep lungful of air and faltered, 'I know, Felipe, I do not doubt you . . . but it is not the time . . .'

He had not tried to repossess her hand, and for that she was grateful. But he was very close. She could smell the damp perspiration on his body, and feared to look into his dark eyes for what she might read there. Her gaze fell on his hand, which clasped the neck of the wine bottle so tightly that the knuckles gleamed white through the sunburned skin.

'As you are a Spanish gentleman and a man of honour, Felipe,' Mariana whispered, 'I know you will understand and respect my feelings . . .'

'I have told you,' he replied, a faint note of anger echoing in his voice, 'that I understand!' He made a visible effort to calm himself, and continued coolly, 'Tell me about the French.'

Mariana began to talk quickly, anxious to turn his mind into new channels. 'The Duchess's house has stood empty these two years, as you know. She went to Madrid—'

'To offer her services to Tio Pepe,' he interrupted her drily, 'in more ways than one! I hear they were graciously accepted.'

'Yesterday,' Mariana continued, 'the French arrived and occupied it. Paco, the muleteer, met them on the road and they confiscated his mules. He came to tell me, so furious I could hardly make out what he said.'

Felipe leaned forward and asked in a tense voice, 'Regiment of the line, or gendarmerie?'

'Dragoons,' she said in a small voice.

Felipe said, 'A—aah . . .' expelling his breath in a long sigh. 'Do they send dragoons after me now?' He gave a chuckle of satisfaction, as though his adversaries had accorded him some honour.

'I don't know whether they've come to hunt for you, or not,' she said quietly. 'Paco says they have wounded with them, as if they have been in battle.'

Felipe narrowed his eyes thoughtfully. 'They are below strength, then.'

'Paco is bad at numbers,' Mariana went on with a sigh. 'But he remembers one officer, riding at the head of the column, who ordered the requisition of the mules. He also saw another officer, who appeared to be very sick, carried on an ox-cart. Some of the others were wounded, all were exhausted, their uniforms torn and dirty. It's true about the uniforms, because later I saw some of them myself when some troopers came into the village. They went into the houses and took all the food they could find.'

'That rabble forced their way into your house?'

he demanded, an angry flush crossing his high cheekbones.

'They came to the door, but I called to the cook to give them the flitch of bacon we had hanging in the kitchen. She did, and they went away.'

'Thieving scum!' Felipe exploded.

'I think they were very hungry,' Mariana ventured.

'All the same, they will pay!' he said harshly. 'If not in coin, then in blood.'

Mariana paled. 'You are not thinking of attacking so many? Even though some are sick and all are tired and hungry, they are well armed.'

'I agree. I myself have only a dozen men here fit to fight, and the French will have turned that mansion into a fortress. We cannot winkle them out there. But they cannot remain barred inside. They will have to send out patrols, foraging parties, such as visited your house. We shall pick them off, a few at a time.'

He spoke very coolly and efficiently, as if talking of a planned game drive and shoot.

Mariana said, 'You talk as though you hunted animals, not men.' Her voice was sober.

'They are animals!' Felipe replied sharply. 'They butcher women and priests. You don't need me to tell you to beware of these men, or that they are dangerous. They will not respect the fact that you are a woman, nor that you are of an old and honourable family. You must take no more risks. You must leave now, and not come here again while they are in this district!'

He leaned forward, his eyes shining with intensity and his voice charged with emotion. 'Though, if I had my wish, you would never leave. You know my heart desires only your favour and the freedom of my country. If those men who came today are able to delay the hour when you will be mine by so much as a minute, I will destroy them utterly. We have waited so long. Nothing now shall keep us apart!'

Mariana's heart began to beat painfully, and she stammered something, hardly knowing what it was.

The man opposite her hesitated, his hawklike features briefly registering a fleeting dissatisfaction. 'If I need to contact you, I'll send José. He knows every goat-path in these hills. José!' he called sharply.

The blanket over the door moved and José entered, squeezing through the narrow aperture with difficulty. When he stood up, his huge, shambling bulk seemed to fill the tiny bivouac. The light of the tallow candle flickered on his bearded face and sinister eye-patch.

Seeing Mariana glance at him a little nervously, the *guerrillero* bared his blackened teeth in a grin and said reassuringly, 'Don't worry, señorita, I have only one eye, but I keep that on the French!'

Felipe laughed and stood up, patting his subordinate's brawny shoulder.

'You will escort Doña Mariana down the hillside as far as the road. Show no lantern. The French may have set a watch.'

Felipe turned back to Mariana and, taking her hand, gracefully kissed her fingertips.

'Next time we meet, I shall ride up to your door on a white horse!' he declared magnificently.

Mariana threw her shawl over her head so that he could not see her face.

As the mule picked its way down the narrow path, led by José, Mariana held tightly to the pommel, and let her mind dwell on Felipe's words.

The war was nearly over. Even if the French made a successful stand now, here in the North, they could not retake the whole of Spain. There would be peace—and Felipe would come down from the hills, take the bath he longed for, call for a barber to cut his long hair, dress in all the finery of a Spanish *hidalgo* and, as he had promised, ride up to her door on a white horse to ask for her hand in marriage.

She would have to accept him. To refuse would be unthinkable. Nor would he accept any refusal. She would not be able to stop her ears to his ardent words of love. She would not be able to plead mourning for her brother, fallen with the flower of Spanish youth at Ocaña, graveyard of the Spanish army. She would no longer have the excuse of the war which ravaged Spain. It would be peacetime, and Felipe would be a national hero.

There would be no tales of cruelty and murder such as clung to the reputation of the guerrilla bands. Only heroic deeds, and a man who had defied cold, starvation and the French for over four years, in the hills. Besides, he was young, handsome, of wealthy and aristocratic family, and he loved her.

But she did not love him. She respected and admired his courage. More than once he had slipped through the fingers of the French, escaping only by his own daring and resourcefulness. She would have given her life in his cause, both as a Spanish patriot, and because he had been Miguel's friend. He could have asked that sacrifice of her at any time, and she would not have hesitated.

But he asked something else—her love. It was a love she could not give him, and the time was nearing inexorably when he would find it out. There are things about which a woman cannot lie. He might not see it in her smile or her eyes, but in the marriage-bed—there he would know the truth, when her arms did not reach out for him or her mouth seek his. She could not pretend that her body yearned for his. She would be cold and unresponsive to the passion of his lovemaking, and it would be as if she had betrayed him.

Mariana sighed.

José, mistaking her distress, hissed in a hoarse whisper, 'It's all right, señorita, I know the way! I know all these paths like the back of my hand. I need no lantern.'

'My father always said you were a smuggler, José,' she whispered back.

In the darkness, she heard him chuckle. Then he said, 'Your father was a good man, and your mother a saint! They were both saints,' he added generously, for good measure.

'My father would have appreciated your high opinion of him, José, but I don't think he would have claimed to be a saint!'

'There are all kinds of saints,' José said comfortably. 'Come on, you idle beast, you devil in a mule's skin!'

The mule had halted obstinately, hoofs planted foursquare.

'Perhaps it senses something,' Mariana whispered.

José grunted. 'Wait there, señorita.' He vanished into the night.

Wait was all she could do, in view of the mule's intransigence. With disconcerting suddenness, the moon came out from behind a cloud. All around, the hills were black and threatening against the ink-blue sky. Mariana looked up, trying to see the stars through the scudding clouds. Perhaps it was going to rain.

There was a sudden, eerie, plaintive cry in the far distance, as if some soul cried out in torment. The mule snorted. It was a wolf, howling to the moon. But more than one kind of wolf hunted the countryside of Spain. Inevitably, the thought drew her back to Felipe, the White Wolf. It was true—men, too, could become wolves in some circumstances. Perhaps the old legends were right.

Shivering, not only from cold, Mariana fought the impulse to call out to José. At last her ear caught the sound of a dislodged pebble rattling away down the steep incline, and a shadowy form emerged from the rocks.

'It's all clear, señorita,' José assured her in his familiar gruff tones. 'Who knows what goes on in a mule's head? You contrary brute, I'll sell your hide to the tanner if you won't budge!'

He hauled at the beast's bridle, and unwillingly the mule moved forward, ears flattened.

'Take care, it bites!' Mariana warned.

'If it bites me, it'll not see its stable again,' growled José. 'Do you hear, you lop-eared monstrosity? You misbegotten abomination of an animal?' There followed some explicit detail of the mule's genealogy which made Mariana both blush and smile, grateful for the darkness.

'Is it true, you were a smuggler?' she asked curiously, when José had run out of invective.

'Over there, in the mountains, every man is a smuggler,' he said blandly.

'But how did you cross without being caught? Aren't there customs posts in the passes?'

'There are paths, if you know them,' José said. 'A man needs only a head for heights and a sure foot.'

They had reached the road at last, and it was now very late.

'You needn't come any further, José,' she told him. 'I have only to follow the road. In twenty minutes, at the most, I shall be home.'

'Don Felipe said I was to see you safe,' José said, as obstinate as the mule he led. 'And he's not a man who likes to have his orders disobeyed. He'll have my ears.'

'Don Felipe said you were to see me safely to the

road, and so you have. Don Felipe would not be pleased if you fell into French hands. He depends on you, José.'

The *guerrillero* hesitated, considering her argument.

'You will make good speed and stop for no reason, nothing at all?' he demanded. 'Were you to see the angel Gabriel standing by the roadside, you would ride by?'

'I promise! Be reasonable, José. I came alone, and can surely find my way home from here.'

'You are a brave woman,' he said after a pause. 'You are a true daughter of your father. Your late brother, God rest his soul, would have been proud of you. He was a fine young man.'

'Yes, he was,' Mariana said.

Miguel lay buried in a shallow grave scratched in the arid soil of central Spain. Brought down in the preliminary onslaught of the French artillery barrage, and limbs and spine shattered as horribly as if he had been broken on the wheel, yet he had still taken fourteen agonising hours to die. She had knelt in the church the day they brought her the news, and sworn, with her hand on the marble tomb of her parents, that the last son of their house had not died in vain and that his blood would be avenged.

'Walk on, you apology for a beast!' José abused the mule, slapping its rump. 'Go with God!' he added kindly to Mariana.

The mule gave a kind of gargling cough, and they lurched forward alone as José turned and vanished into the hillside. The mule was on the road home, and knew it. As it drew nearer to its warm stable, its ambling pace quickened, and it broke into a jarring trot.

Mariana realised they must be approaching the humped stone bridge over the river. She could hear the gurgling of the water racing down from the hills over the boulder-strewn bed. A dark form, with outstretched arms, stood by the road, and the mule snorted and shied. But it was only a wayside Calvary.

The timbre of the mule's hoofbeats changed from dull thud to echoing clatter as they crossed the bridge. On the further side they passed by some pines. The wind stirred the tree-tops, bringing their scent on the air, and the mule blew through its nostrils at the changing shadows. Mariana pulled on the reins and halted, listening. The clouds scudded furiously across the sky, and the pines sighed and whispered. A storm was coming. She must make haste to get home. She took the reins and urged the mule on.

'*Arrêtez!*'

The loud cry broke through the night like a sudden clap of thunder. The shadows among the pines became alive, swarming like the veiled monsters of a nightmare around mule and rider. Mariana shrieked. The mule leaped forward, snorting with fright, and was roughly restrained by a hand which seized the bridle. The masking cloth was pulled from a horn lantern, and Mariana threw up her hand to shield her eyes from the sudden light, as the lantern was raised on high and shone into her face.

'Sergeant Beaudoin! See here!' called a hoarse, excited voice in French. 'We've caught ourselves a pigeon!'

A burly shape pushed forward and grasped the horn lantern from the man who had spoken, swinging it across Mariana's face.

'No pigeon,' growled a new voice. 'A nightingale, boys. A pretty nightingale—and perhaps she'll sing for us! Bring her along. She can sing her song to the captain!'

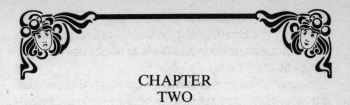

CHAPTER
TWO

As THE lantern light flickered erratically on the uniforms about her, Mariana knew without a doubt that she had fallen into the hands of those very dragoons of whose presence she had ridden to warn Felipe. She was hustled through the night, terror-stricken and powerless, and bundled at last through the doorway of what was, she realised amidst her panic, the great country house of the absent *afrancesada* Duchess.

But what a different arrival from the last time she had been here. Then the entrance hall had been ablaze with light. Not only two or three candles in wine-bottles barely illuminated it. The ceiling above was lost in the shadows, the magnificent staircase was only a dim outline in the background and she could make out nothing at all in the further corners.

The sergeant, Beaudoin, had vanished, presumably to inform his superior officer of the capture. The other men formed themselves into a ring round her, pressing their bodies close against her, whispering and laughing together. Her nostrils were assailed by the powerful odour of sweat and sour wine, and she felt herself struggling for breath.

Suddenly, a hand reached out and dragged the shawl from her head. The rough movement pulled loose the pins in her hair and it tumbled down in long chestnut curls.

Someone seized a candle and pushed it almost into her face, so that she gasped and started back. Another unseen hand grasped the long locks of hair and jerked back her head, and Mariana cried out in pain.

The man with the candle snarled through his teeth. 'A beauty!'

'I found her!' claimed a truculent voice. 'I say she's mine!'

'And I say we draw straws for her!' another voice contradicted him fiercely. 'We were all there when she was found.'

'You hold your tongue, Michel Boucher, you wouldn't know what to do with a woman like this, even if you had one,' was the gratuitously insulting response.

'Lads, lads,' urged a peacemaker, 'there's no need to be quarrelling over her, we are all comrades and used to sharing—'

Mariana tore her head free, and threw herself at a gap in the circle about her which had opened up as they began to squabble among themselves.

'Watch out, stop her!' yelled Michel Boucher. Rendered doubly aggressive by the taunting of his companions, he lunged and caught her roughly by the arm, dragging her back.

Mariana twisted and struggled. In her despair and terror, she fought with a ferocity she herself would not have suspected lay within her, clawing and scratching at his face like a wild thing, and wriggling and kicking in his arms until he was forced to release his grip to throw up his hand to protect his own face.

'Help me!' he shouted. 'I can't hold the hellcat, she's trying to scratch my eyes out!'

The others ran to his aid, but Mariana wrenched herself free so violently that she left her would-be restrainers holding nothing but shreds of her gown, torn away in the struggle.

Suddenly, above all the noise and shouting, a new voice made itself heard, yelling more loudly than any of the others and swearing vigorously.

'Release her, I say, damn you! Release her!'

The men fell back. The clutching hands let her go, and she was left, panting and dishevelled, her long hair tumbled about her face, her fingers plucking at her ruined gown, trying to drag the tattered material across the bare white skin of her bosom.

'Well, Beaudoin?' demanded a sharply incisive and angry voice. 'Is this your spy?'

'Yes, Captain Dupré, sir.' The sergeant elbowed his way forward through the now silent circle of men and, taking Mariana not ungently by the wrist, pulled her forward. 'I know she's only a peasant girl, but why should she be coming down the hillside by mule, at night, alone? Peasants lock themselves indoors at night. Frightened of spooks, half of them.'

Mariana was beginning to gather her wits. She pushed back her hair with one hand, drew herself up with dignity and stared challengingly into the darkness towards the unseen owner of the voice of authority.

There was a movement at the foot of the great staircase, and a tall, shadowy form loomed up, pausing just beyond the ring of candlelight, so that she still could not see him properly. She could make out only the pale oval of a face, darker smudges indicating features. She felt a prickle of fear, as if the figure beyond the candlelight were somehow less than human.

'This is no peasant girl,' the voice said softly. 'Who are you?' These last words were addressed to her curtly, in Spanish.

'I am Doña Mariana Alvarez de las Fuentes,' Mariana returned icily, 'and I have been treated barbarously by your men. I demand an apology—and that you release me immediately!'

'My sergeant says you are a spy,' the voice retorted, unimpressed.

'He is a fool.' Mariana tossed her loose chestnut curls dismissively.

'No—he is a shrewd man, and I respect his judgment. Why were you riding out alone, at night?'

'I was returning from a visit to the next village,' Mariana snapped. She wished she could see him. It was becoming increasingly difficult to maintain a confident tone when conversing with a figure as insubstantial as a ghost. She did not know how much longer she could cling to the tone of haughty disdain. 'I am still waiting for your apology!'

'Wait as long as you like,' was the brusque rejoinder. There was the barest pause, and he added drily, 'Pretty girls, who ride out alone at night, in wild country swarming with soldiers, ought not to be surprised if they find themselves obliged to surrender their virtue with every mile of the way!' The shadowy figure turned away. 'Lock her in one of the bedrooms, sergeant!' he ordered Beaudoin. 'These men are to go nowhere near her. I don't want any men of mine fighting each other over one Spanish girl. They can save their energies to defend the soil of France! I'll see her in the morning.'

He stepped back into the shadows, even the indefinable outline of his form vanishing so abruptly that, instinctively, Mariana's hand twitched as if to make the sign of the Cross. She stopped herself just in time, furious with her own superstitious imagination, and telling herself angrily that he had been but a French officer like many others she had seen.

Before she had time to think further, she found herself escorted firmly up the staircase by the sergeant, bundled into a room, the door locked behind her.

As Beaudoin had taken the candle away with him, Mariana was left in total darkness, but after feeling her way forward cautiously, she struck her hand against the corner-post of a fourposter bed. She scrambled up on to the smooth satin coverlet, alone with far from comforting thoughts. She had no idea whether anyone had seen her brought here, and did not know which possibility alarmed her most: that Felipe would not discover what had become of her, or that he would—and take drastic action.

In the meantime she had but a few hours to concoct a convincing story to tell Captain Dupré on the morrow. Mariana sighed and sank her head despondently into her hands. How to face a man who had appeared so far only as a disembodied voice in the darkness? All she knew of him for certain was that he spoke good Spanish, and was unlikely to be guided in his conduct by notions of gentlemanly behaviour. What did they do with spies? At least he did not know that she spoke French, and it would be far better that he did not discover this fact too soon.

She lay down, resting her head on the feather pillows, fighting back the hot tears of shock, and tried to sleep. As she did so an odd, muffled noise struck her ear, and she sat up again with a start, listening intently.

There it was again. It sounded like a moan, coming from the next room. Petrified, Mariana threw the coverlet over her head, as she had done when a child and the wind rattled at the nursery shutters, and fell asleep at last, crouched in the bed with only the tip of her nose poking out from the covers for air.

She was woken by the sunlight streaming through the louvred window shutter, and sat up, not surprisingly somewhat stiff, to look around her.

To her amazement, she was in the most splendid bedroom she had ever seen. The walls were hung with primrose silk, and the ceiling painted all over with plump cherubs, proffering floral wreaths towards a central scene of an enamoured Cupid, discovering a pinkly naked and voluptuous sleeping Psyche.

With the sunlight of the new day, and in these luxurious surroundings, many of her fears of the previous night shrank to manageable proportions. Mariana slipped out of bed and walked slowly round the room, opening drawers and doors. The wardrobe was filled with expensive gowns, the drawers with exquisite linen. All the accessories of the dressing-table were of silver. Without a doubt, she was in the absent Duchess's own bedroom. Mariana took the silver stopper from a crystal perfume-bottle and sniffed. French perfume, smuggled perhaps across the Pyrenees, by José, or someone like him.

But there was no water in the painted, gilded porcelain basin or the jug. Mariana wondered when someone was going to remember her. She would like to wash and, besides, she was hungry.

As she stood there, she heard a woman's voice, calling out loudly on the floor below. It had not occurred to Mariana that there might be any other woman in the house, and she pressed her ear to the door panels, trying to catch some of the words.

A torrent of Spanish rewarded her, coming nearer up the great staircase towards this room, and in an ever more familiar, if unexpected, voice—that of her own maid, Juana.

'Juana!' Mariana screamed, beating on the door

panels with her clenched fists. 'Juana, I'm here!'

'Doña Mariana!' cried a voice, and there was a patter of feet. 'These wretches won't let me see you! Open the door, you French pig, do you hear me?' continued the voice furiously. 'You scoundrel, you rogue, you son of a bawd—open this door and let me go to my lady!'

'Oh, for pity's sake,' groaned a resigned male voice—Sergeant Beaudoin's—'let some saint protect me from screeching women! I joined up to get away from one, and now I'm burdened with this creature. Hold your tongue, you ill-favoured shrew! I'll unlock the door. Let me get by, will you?' he added in a stentorian roar.

'You great oaf, you thick-skulled murdering bandit, give me that key!'

There was a crash and a clatter.

'Now you see what you've done, you harridan? I've dropped the cursed thing. Get out of my way!'

As on the sergeant's side the conversation was undertaken in French, and on Juana's in Spanish, it was doubtful that either understood exactly what the other said, but the general meaning of both was quite clear.

The door flew open, and a stocky peasant woman burst into the room and flung her arms about Mariana.

'There you are, my poor lady! I told this idiot I wouldn't leave till I'd seen you.' Juana uttered a piercing shriek. 'What's happened to your gown? It's torn to shreds. What have they done to you?' And Juana leapt at Beaudoin and fetched the unfortunate sergeant a resounding box on the ears which must have made his head ring. 'You dog!'

'No, no, Juana, calm down, it's all right!' Mariana urged, pulling the infuriated maid away. 'Sergeant, it's all right, really!' she added placatingly to the aggrieved Beaudoin.

'You listen to me,' said Beaudoin, breathing heavily and rubbing his ear. 'Captain Dupré says he'll see you in twenty minutes. Twenty. Understand?' Beaudoin held up the fingers of his right hand four times. 'I'll leave this harpy with you and she can help you to dress. Captain Dupré says you can help yourself to one of the dresses in the cupboard here.' Beaudoin strode to the wardrobe and wrenched it open. 'One of these, understand?'

Juana snorted. 'Ape!' she said shortly, when the sergeant had departed.

'The poor man's doing his best. Juana, do you think they'd let me have some water to wash?'

Juana ran after the sergeant and could be heard shouting at him as he went downstairs.

'All right, all right. *Agua, agua!* I understand!' Beaudoin roared in reply.

'He's not very bright, if you ask me,' said Juana on her return. 'But I think he's getting to understand me.'

'How did you know I was here, Juana?'

'Paco, the muleteer, has been watching this house, hoping for a chance to get back the mules they stole from him. But, alas, it wasn't until this morning he had the wit to come and tell us whom it was the wretches had locked up here. I flew here as if my feet had wings!'

'Did Paco send word—did he tell anyone else?' Mariana asked cautiously, lowering her voice and glancing at the door.

Juana's voice sank to a dramatic whisper. 'Those who should know, will know!' she hissed mysteriously.

It was a far from satisfactory answer. Mariana drummed her fingertips impatiently on the dressing-table and frowned.

Juana had gone to the wardrobe to inspect the gowns, and now sighed. 'Just look, Doña Mariana, what beautiful gowns the poor Duchess had to leave behind. I remember when she left. She took only three carriages of trunks and boxes with her.'

'Only three?' Mariana said crossly. 'Perhaps she thought King Joseph would buy her all new gowns from Paris!'

'What will you wear, señorita?'

Footsteps and a chink of china indicated that the water had arrived and had been set down outside the door. While Juana went to bring it in, Mariana sorted thoughtfully through the wardrobe.

'I shall wear this, Juana,' she said.

It was a costume in the style called 'Maja'. It had originated with the girls of Madrid, but the ladies of the aristocracy had been quick to perceive the sensual charm of the tight bodice, the skirt of tiered lace flounces, the low neck and bare arms, and the lace mantilla, and to add at least one such gown to their own wardrobes.

'You don't want to give these Frenchmen any ideas,' said Juana darkly. 'They've no respect for decent women as it is.'

'Don't worry,' Mariana told her calmly. 'I'm sure the only idea lodged in Captain Dupré's head is that I am a spy. I shall wear this dress, Juana, just because it is a Spanish dress. This is my country . . . he is an invader who came here with a foreign army to impose a foreign king on us. I shall lose no opportunity to remind him of it!'

Brave words, but they concealed a rising nausea of apprehension. Mariana sat before the mirror to allow Juana to brush out her thick chestnut hair. She stared moodily at her own reflection, forcing down the nervous trembling which threatened to make her physically sick.

People said she was beautiful. She herself had always thought her mouth too wide. Her large hazel eyes were her best feature. Otherwise she was too slightly built for Spanish taste. Miguel had always teased her by calling her his little scarecrow of a sister. But even he, she knew, had boasted to his friends of his sister's beauty. But what had that beauty and her brother's boasts done but win her the attentions of a man she could never love? Beauty was a curse. Many a time, especially of late, she had looked in a mirror like this one, and heartily wished herself the plainest young woman in Spain.

None the less, she would make herself present-able for her interrogator, if only to bolster her own flagging morale. In the little time allotted to them,

Mariana and Juana did their best, Mariana helping herself freely to the Duchess's perfume and lip rouge. Juana swept back her hair smoothly and secured it with pins in a thick knot at the nape of her neck, carefully arranging a few strands in a fringe across her forehead and twisting a flat curl in front of each ear. In a drawer, they found a silver inlaid tortoiseshell comb, which Juana placed carefully into the knot of hair, draping the lace mantilla over it.

There was a knock at the door. 'Are you ready, mademoiselle?' asked Beaudoin through the panels.

It was time. The nausea vanished. Mariana remembered how she had once heard a celebrated bullfighter tell his admiring audience that this was how it was, before he stepped into the arena. Beforehand he felt fear, but once on the sand facing his snorting adversary, only calm and determination. Mariana took a last quick look in the mirror and draped the lace mantilla a little more decorously over her bare shoulders.

'Wait for me here, quietly!' she instructed her maid as she stepped out into the corridor for her own private duel.

'Don't worry, señorita, I shall lock myself in!' declared Juana, rolling her eyes suspiciously at Beaudoin and brandishing the key under his nose.

Beaudoin gave her a look of disgust. 'I don't know what you're worried about,' he said. 'You're safe enough. I'd sooner face the British guns. Any

man brave enough to get into your bed ought to be
given a medal.'

Mariana followed him downstairs. In the great
hall, however, she stopped and gasped in dismay.

Daylight revealed the extent of the depredations
left by the Duchess's uninvited guests. The whole
area was littered with all kinds of impedimenta.
The polished floor, which had once shone like a
mirror, was scuffed and muddied. Curtains had
been torn from the windows, the gilded, branched
candelabra from the walls ripped out, presumably,
as booty. But the thing which distressed her most
was that someone had slashed the great oil paintings, too large to be removed as trophies, in a
vicious and meaningless attack. One, a Velázquez,
hung in tatters.

'Who has done that?' demanded Mariana, pointing accusingly at the ruined paintings and forget-
ting she had intended to conceal her knowledge
of French. 'I shall complain to Captain Dupré.
It is his responsibility to prevent such—such
crimes!'

Beaudoin followed her gaze, but only shrugged.
'Better paintings than heads,' he said phlegmati-
cally. If he thought it strange that she spoke
French, he did not show any sign of it. 'My old
granny used to go along to watch the heads roll on
the Place de la Bastille, in 'ninety-three. Loved it,
she did. Used to take her knitting along with her.'
He pointed to a door. 'Through there.'

Silenced by Beaudoin's sanguine recall of past
horrors, and by her own imminent interrogation,

Mariana opened the door a little tremulously, and stepped inside.

It had formerly been a morning-room, and was bathed now in the pale yellow of early sunlight. The tall, narrow windows had been flung open to let in the sweet air and reveal the greenery of the gardens. Most of the furniture had been pushed back roughly against the walls to leave a clear space in the centre for a huge walnut desk, which must have been brought in here from elsewhere in the house. On it stood a tray with a pot of hot coffee, bread and a bowl of oranges. In one corner, a folding camp-bed had been set up. With so many luxuriously appointed bedrooms in the house, she could not think why, unless the captain liked a Spartan life.

At that moment there was a movement in the far corner, and someone swore quietly, but with great feeling, in French.

Beaudoin had brought her too soon. The captain, stripped naked to the waist, was bending over a basin of water and splashing his face and shoulders. He had his back towards her, and she was not certain whether he knew she had entered. In any event, he took no notice, continuing with his ablutions. Mariana was left to study his back apprehensively.

His skin was burned by the sun to the golden bronze which fair skins turn, and beneath it she could see the muscles stretched taut. As she watched, he poured water from his cupped hands over his head. It ran down in shining rivulets over the bare skin, down the length of the spine, to where a wide swathe of dark-stained, white linen bandage was bound tightly around his ribs, and she realised with shock that every movement which pulled at that glistening, sunburned skin, flexing the muscles beneath, caused him pain.

Abruptly he straightened up with a sharp grunt, put out his left hand and, without looking round, ordered, 'Towel!'

A towel, embroidered with the crest of the absent Duchess, lay on a chair. Mariana picked it up and handed it to him. As his fingers touched hers, he gave a slight start and glanced down.

'Oh, it's you,' he said in Spanish, still without turning round. 'I thought it was Beaudoin.'

He began to rub his hair dry, turning towards her as he did. Mariana backed away nervously, though it seemed a matter of total indifference to him whether she watched him or not. He tossed down the damp towel carelessly on the silken seat of a chair, and reached for the shirt draped over the chairback. For the first time, Mariana saw his face . . . and gave a little gasp.

It was a face which had once been handsome. The widely set cheekbones appeared prominent, perhaps because the cheeks were a little sunken, but above them the grey eyes were clear and sharp. The nose was somewhat on the Roman model, and the mouth sensitively drawn and scored on either side by little lines, as if—once upon a time—the owner had laughed a lot. Once, but no longer, for the right side of the face was marked by a horrendous, half-healed wound, puckering up the skin and reaching up into the hairline above the ear. It was as if some great animal had reached out and clawed savagely at his face, scraping a furrow almost to the bone, and scarring him for life.

For the rest, he was a much younger man than she had anticipated, or, indeed, would have liked; taller than most Frenchmen, and with close-cropped brown hair, streaked and bleached by the sun, rumpled now by the rough towelling into a boyish disorder. But it was the scar which took her eye, drawing her gaze to it irresistibly.

He looked up and saw her staring at him, wide-eyed, her horror and revulsion plainly written on her face.

'What's the matter?' he asked sarcastically. 'Do I turn your stomach? You should have seen it at the beginning. It was worse.'

Mariana ran her tongue over her dry lips. 'W-what caused it?' she stammered.

'The English have invented a new kind of exploding shell—or one of their officers has. A Colonel Shrapnel. It is very effective. More effective, anyway, than those peculiar rockets of theirs that they insist on firing at us, and always seem to land among their own men!' The good side of his face twisted into a wry half-smile. 'I was fortunate. I was shielded from the main blast. The surgeon saved my eyesight and dug a lump of metal the size of your pretty little fist out of my ribs.'

He began to struggle awkwardly into his coat.

'Shall—shall—I fetch your sergeant?' Mariana

whispered, embarrassed by the obvious effort this simple action cost him.

'No!' he said curtly. 'I can manage. Sit down, señorita, and join me for breakfast.' He indicated the tray on the desk.

The whole interview was not turning out at all as Mariana had expected. Nor, for that matter, was Captain Dupré. For one thing, despite his dreadful injuries and the uncertainty of the situation, he seemed in better humour than the night before, though his relatively good humour was probably only a fragile veneer, and very little would be needed to destroy it.

Steam wafted up from the coffee-pot. It smelled delicious, and Mariana's hunger reawakened.

'Pour it out,' he ordered her. 'You can manage it better than I can.'

As she did so, he lowered himself slowly and stiffly into the chair on the further side of the desk and leaned back, stretching out his long legs in the tight white breeches. Perhaps it was truer to say the colour of the breeches was near to grey, for they were plentifully streaked with dry mud. His green coat and white waistcoat, both unbuttoned, were likewise begrimed. The state of his shirt linen also left a great deal to be desired and she could now see that he needed a shave. For all he was in uniform, he looked scarcely more presentable than Felipe, in the hills. There was something else, too, about him, which reminded her of Felipe. It was a quality, invisible and intangible, yet of which she could not fail to be aware: the quality of a man tempered like steel in the furnace of war.

Though very nervous, she managed to pour out the coffee for them both without spilling any, and then sat down to meet the scrutiny of the grey eyes which had been watching her thoughtfully all the while.

Mariana wondered uncomfortably just what he was thinking. But there was no way of reading what lay behind that intelligent, level gaze. As she stared back into his face, as boldly as she could, she realised that she was almost unaware now of the scar, because the grey eyes dominated it, almost relegating it to insignificance.

Like butterflies borne on a storm wind, the most inconsequential and inappropriate of thoughts flicker through the mind at moments of great stress. Mariana found herself thinking: 'He has very fine eyes and he is still very handsome, once you get over the shock of that scar. Before he was wounded, he must have been very attractive. Women would have liked him. I expect he liked them.'

A tremor of a new kind of unease ran through her, and she pushed her chair back a little to put more distance between them.

'You have a steady hand,' he observed suddenly, and she jumped at the unexpected sound of his voice. 'In your situation, I should have poured coffee all over the desk.'

'My conscience is clear!' Mariana retorted.

'I should be more inclined to believe that were you shaking like a leaf. Contrary to popular belief, innocence usually betrays itself by its confusion, guilt by its calm.'

'You speak like a lawyer,' she said distastefully.

'Do I?' he asked. 'I once studied the law—but it wasn't for me. Drink your coffee, señorita,' he added pleasantly, indicating her cup. 'My sergeant made it. He makes excellent coffee. He once had a small café in the Faubourg St Germain. Alas, it was presided over by his scolding wife. One day, he took off his apron and went out and enlisted.'

'He and my maid argued . . .' Mariana said, not knowing quite how to reply.

'Do you think I couldn't hear it? They made a devil of a noise.' He began to sip at the hot coffee.

Mariana, still more disconcerted by his informality, said, 'He spoke French, and she spoke Spanish, but it didn't prevent them quarrelling.'

'Well, I suppose two people do not need a common language to quarrel—or to make love,' he returned unexpectedly. The grey eyes rested on her, the look in them not entirely attributable to mockery.

Mariana flushed. 'You speak excellent Spanish, Captain!'

'And you, señorita,' he retorted, 'do you by any chance speak French?'

Mariana hesitated. Had he heard her speaking French to the sergeant? 'Why do you ask?' she temporised.

'Because you are a young lady of good family, and I assume you have had some kind of high-minded education.'

He would discover the truth eventually, probably from Beaudoin. But, in the meantime, there was no need to make him a present of any information. Mariana, ignoring the dangers of lying unnecessarily under interrogation, said aloofly, 'I regret, my education did not include French.'

'Then it was incomplete,' he observed in a tone of irritating complacency.

He set down his cup and, picking up the bread, broke off a piece of the crust. He had well-shaped hands, the fingers long and slender, the nails cut short and very clean. The contrast between this and the sorry state of his clothes could not have been more marked, and told its own story.

With a display of those practical manners which sometimes startle those who sit at table with the French, he dunked his bread unconcernedly in his coffee and observed, a little indistinctly, 'I've been in this country long enough not only to learn Spanish, but to discover—to my cost and often to my despair—that no respectable Spanish girl crosses the street without some hatchet-faced duenna in tow. I never knew a race of women so well guarded. You might as well be Turks. So you see, I am very curious to know just what you were doing last night, out and alone.'

'I have already told you,' Mariana snapped. 'How dare you ask me questions? Your men treated me unforgivably!'

'You weren't hurt, and you seem to have recovered.' His tone was unsympathetic.

'Not hurt? How do you treat your women in

France, may I ask? I shouldn't be surprised to hear that you beat them! Look!' Dramatically, she stretched out one bare arm towards him so that he could see the purple print of Michel Boucher's thumb marking the soft white flesh. 'What do you call that?' she demanded.

'I call it a very pretty arm!' he replied promptly. 'Consider yourself lucky to escape with a bruise or two. It was entirely your own doing. You should have stayed at home, like a good girl, and not gone wandering about in circumstances which even you must see court, well, let us say "adventure", to save your blushes! And I might add that one or two of my men have gained a few scratches. For a young lady so gently bred, you fought like a gipsy!'

Enraged, Mariana leapt to her feet, her hazel eyes blazing with fury. 'You defend your men? But for your own arrival on the scene, your men would have—' She broke off, scarlet-faced, and sat down abruptly. 'Only your arrival prevented an assault upon my honour!' she concluded in a muffled voice.

He raised his eyebrows. 'Then you should be grateful I arrived in time! Show a little gratitude. Thank me,' he suggested.

'Thank you?' Mariana cried. 'I owe you not the slightest thanks!'

'Quite right. You don't. I didn't rescue you for the sake of your honour. Alas, that—interesting a subject though it is—is none of my concern. My reason was simply that one woman among so many men can cause havoc. Sufficient women keep soldiers happy,' he added laconically. 'One woman is always bad for discipline.'

Mariana, rendered speechless, glared at him, her eyes flashing.

'Of course, señorita,' he said, 'one man and one woman is a different story. Perhaps you think my injuries render me temporarily *hors de combat* in the matter of love. We could find out.'

'You insult me,' Mariana said icily.

'I insult you . . .' he repeated slowly. '*I* insult *you*. You treacherous little liar, you insult me! Do you think I am to be fooled by a pretty face and a fine display of outraged virtue?'

His voice was very cold and quiet and seemed to freeze every muscle in Mariana's body. Even the note of taunting mockery had vanished. The grey eyes were like ice on a winter dawn.

Mariana's throat constricted and she swallowed with difficulty. 'I don't know what you mean,' she managed to utter.

'Don't you? I think you do.' He stood up and came round the desk to stand over her. Mariana cowered back in her seat.

'What's the matter?' he asked softly, but the voice was still that which had come from the shadows the night before, and it chilled her blood. 'Do you think *I* might beat you? I have never struck a woman, *querida*, and I don't intend to start now, so you needn't fix me with such round eyes.' He leaned back against the desk and rested his hands on the edge. 'You will not deny there are bands of guerrilla fighters out there, up in the hills?'

'They are Spanish patriots!' Mariana returned defiantly. 'They fight for Spain's freedom, and my heart is with them! But *I* was not,' she added firmly.

'One band at least must be very near to here. Last night I saw the light of their fires on the skyline. You came from that direction,' he added calmly.

'I came by the road,' Mariana said quickly.

'One of their leaders,' he went on, ignoring her interruption, 'is known by the *nom de guerre* of the White Wolf. Perhaps you have heard of him?'

'Yes, I've heard of him,' Mariana answered carefully. 'All Spain has heard of him. You French have been trying to capture him for over four years. Now you never will!' she added unwisely.

'Why?' he returned swiftly. 'Because you think the war is over, and there will soon be none of us left in Spain?' With a sudden movement he reached out and took her chin in his fingers, forcing her to look up into his face. 'That man,' he said grimly, 'is a cold-blooded, merciless and sadistic killer, and if I could have had the opportunity to snare that wolf and nail his pelt to the church door, then this soldier of France, at least, would be leaving Spain well-contented.'

Mariana twisted her head free of his grip. 'And the French?' she flung at him. 'They do not shoot unarmed men? They do not burn villages?'

He paused, then said quietly, 'It is in the nature of war that these things happen. They are always to be regretted, but they will always happen where men fight. But a man like the White Wolf is worse than the beast whose name he has adopted. The wolf kills from necessity—but he kills for pleasure.'

Mariana opened her mouth to cry out that all he said was a lie, that Felipe was a Spanish patriot, a Spanish gentleman and a man of honour. Just in time, she managed to stop herself. She bit her lips till they hurt, and stared challengingly at him, her white bosom in the low-cut bodice of the Maja dress heaving with suppressed emotion.

'And as for you,' her opponent said, and there was something about the way he said 'you', which made it far worse than any insult, and Mariana felt her cheeks burn. 'You rode out into those hills to meet someone. Let me tell you frankly—if I had any evidence that your rendezvous was with that particular fiend, I would have Beaudoin take you outside here this minute, and shoot you out of hand!'

Mariana stared at him, as frozen as a statue. His manner relaxed a little and he pushed himself away from the desk, and, to her great relief, moved a few steps away from her.

'As it is, I have a better use for you,' he said, and her heart leapt up in fear again.

Glancing at her alarmed face, he added insolently, 'You expect a further assault upon your honour, do you? It grieves me to disappoint you. Your use to me is this: first, when whoever you met with last night learns I have you safe here, he may be tempted out of his lair, and into mine.'

'What makes you think he will come?' Mariana's

voice sounded to her own ears little better than a croak.

He gave her a dry smile. 'I have met you. You are young, beautiful, and passionate. Whoever he was, this man you met last night, he is more to you than just a "Spanish patriot". He is a lover. One does not need to be French to deduce that! If *I* were your lover—' he paused. 'Were such fortune mine, I would try to rescue you. If he is any kind of a man, he will do the same.'

'Second,' he continued, when she did not answer, 'while I have you, he will not play his game of picking off my men, one by one. He would not risk that pretty white neck of yours. They move stealthily, your friends. A knife in the dark is their trademark. But not while I have you, *querida*, not while I have you!'

'I understand,' Mariana snapped defiantly, 'I am your hostage!'

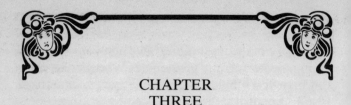

CHAPTER
THREE

MARIANA CONTRIVED to leave the room with dignity, only a rustle of lace flounces as she passed through the door betraying her inner agitation. She did not look back, although she could sense his eyes following her.

Outside, in the great entrance hall, the door to his room closed, she drew a deep breath.

'Stay in the house,' had been his parting instructions. 'Keep away from my men and don't attempt to step outside. If you do, I shall have you locked in your room upstairs—which you will find very tedious and unpleasant. And change that dress! Find one which is less revealing of your considerable charms. I cannot have you wandering about so distractingly attired.'

'I'm sure,' Mariana had managed to say in a barely controlled voice, 'that I don't wish to do anything to disturb the peace of mind of your men!'

'I don't know about theirs,' he said in a forthright tone. 'It certainly disturbs mine!'

'Impudent wretch!' she muttered now. But at least she had said nothing to betray Felipe. She glanced up and saw a trooper, stationed in the main doorway watching her intently. He was small and wiry, with little button eyes that fixed her with a spiteful and cunning expression. The chinstrap of his helmet did not disguise the fact that his face was scored by long, recently inflicted, scratches— Michel Boucher, harbouring a grudge against her, and biding his time. She did not need to be told to stay away from that soldier. Mariana stared at him coldly, and had the satisfaction of seeing him avoid her eye.

At that moment the gold and white double doors to the ballroom swung open. Beaudoin stepped into the hall, and the sight of his honest, red face raised her spirits slightly.

'He's through with you, is he?' he observed to Mariana, a comment which brought forth a salacious chuckle from Boucher.

'Got something to say, have you?' the sergeant asked him, with no very kindly glint in his eye, and Boucher reddened and moved away.

Mariana proceeded on her way upstairs, well pleased, at least, at Boucher's discomfiture, though having little else to cheer her thoughts.

'Help me out of this dress!' she ordered Juana sharply, on reaching her room.

The maid unhooked the dress and, as it rustled to the floor about her feet, Mariana went on morosely, 'I can't imagine anything worse than being shut up in this house and having to take orders from that man. A miserable little lawyer's clerk who has scrambled and fought his way to a position of authority, thanks to a uniform and the ambitions of the Bonaparte family!'

'A fine-looking man, all the same, that captain,' Juana observed, a far-away look in her eyes. 'He came to see what was amiss, when I was arguing my way in here. He spoke to me kindly enough, and in a beautiful Castilian, and told the sergeant to let me go up.'

'I want no kindnesses from him!' Mariana said fiercely. 'I feel like Daniel in the lions' den. At least he had an angel or two to help him!'

'And so shall you, my pretty one,' Juana assured her soothingly. 'For Don Felipe will not—'

'Hush!' Mariana clapped her hand over the maid's mouth. 'Never mention that name, never! There are ears everywhere here. Anyone might be listening and most of these men probably have a few words of Spanish.'

For the rest of the morning she remained in the Duchess's bedroom, staring disconsolately at the painted ceiling, and gradually growing to hate the simpering expression of the sleeping Psyche.

Towards noon, Juana went downstairs, returning with a bowl of vegetable soup which proved delicious, and some fresh goat-cheese. Even in adversity, it seemed, the French were maintaining tenaciously their devotion to the culinary art.

'The kitchen,' said Juana severely, 'seems to be the only place anyone's organised properly at all—although, to my mind, some of those cooking-pots have seen a good deal of campaigning, and need a good scrub out.'

'Don't tell me, Juana,' Mariana said, scraping

out the last of the soup. 'I'd rather not know.'

'We're in for a storm.' The maid went to close the window. 'Only feel how oppressive it's become, and there's not a breath of wind out there. I swear I heard thunder not five minutes ago. I'm going down to the chapel, and if those rogues have left so much as a stub of candle in it, I'll light it to Saint Barbara, to keep us safe from the lightning, when it comes.'

There was indeed a storm brewing, but candles would not protect them from it, Mariana thought.

Juana was gathering up Mariana's soup dish and plate, both of which were of fine porcelain, and with the ducal crest. 'Help themselves to anything!' she observed with a disapproving sniff.

'I don't mind. I'd rather eat off china than a tin plate,' Mariana said.

'Just you lie down there and sleep for a little,' Juana instructed her. 'It's too close and sticky to move. Even that donkey of a sergeant is asleep in the entrance hall, with his boots off, and his great big feet up on one of the chairs.'

Mariana lay down on the bed in her chemise and flounced petticoat. 'Stop calling poor Beaudoin names,' she murmured sleepily. 'He's quite a nice man . . . nicer than his captain, anyway!'

A silence, the silence of siesta, compounded by the stillness preceding the approaching storm, fell over everything. Mariana dozed and then, suddenly, opened her eyes wide. Clearly, in the silence, came again that moaning from the next room, just as she had heard it during the night. There was someone in there, someone in distress.

Mariana slipped cautiously from the bed and opened the door. Nothing stirred outside, only a faint snoring floated upstairs from Sergeant Beaudoin, slumbering in the hall below.

Over a chair lay a large, fringed, silk shawl. Mariana snatched it up and threw it over her bare shoulders, knotting it over her breast. Then she crept along the empty corridor to the door of the next room, and put her ear to the panels. She pushed down the wrought gilt handle, and the door swung noiselessly open.

The room was shuttered and in semi-darkness, and smelled stale.

'Faugh!' Mariana muttered, and pulled the window open, throwing back one side of the shutters.

The afternoon sun entered together with the fresh air, and she turned at the sound of a movement from the bed. A man lay there, tossing on the pillows restlessly. He did not speak, and Mariana gathered enough courage to approach him.

He was very young, but his skin was yellowed and stretched like parchment across the bones of his face. His eyes, glazed and dull, stared up at her unseeingly. His lips were dry and cracked, but his forehead was moist with sweat and the pillows damp and stained. The sickly stench of fever struck her nostrils.

Mariana's first instinct was to step back hastily from the bedside, with her hand over her mouth and nose. To approach fever victims was both rash and foolish. When fever entered a house, its occupants fled; besides which, this was obviously a French officer.

But as she looked down at him, so young and so helpless, it was as if she saw her own brother, Miguel, as he had been in the long hours of a final agony so terrible that even a passing victorious French officer had been moved to give him brandy to ease his pain.

Near by was a washstand with a bowl of water. Mariana snatched up one of the little towels with the ducal monogram, and soaking it in the water, squeezed it out and laid it over the sick man's forehead. She looked about frantically for drinking water, though some people said, she knew, that fever victims ought not to be given water, only broth. As she resoaked the towel, there was a movement from the doorway behind her.

'What are you doing here?' asked a quiet voice, and she spun round to find Dupré.

He came further into the room, and the door swung closed behind him.

'This is no place for you. Go on,' he jerked his head towards the door behind him. 'Get out of here!'

'Why is nobody looking after him?' she demanded in a low voice, pointing at the man on the bed. 'Is this how you treat your sick?'

He took a quick stride towards her and seized her roughly by the arm. 'I said, get away from him!' he rasped.

'Take your hand off me!' Mariana flared at him, all her pent-up anger boiling over. 'How dare you touch me, you French murderer!' In her fury, she struck out at him with her fist as hard as she could.

He gave a gasp and, releasing her, stepped back. She saw him turn pale and realised that her blow had struck against his injured ribs.

Mariana's hand flew to her mouth. 'Oh—I'm so sorry,' she faltered. Instinctively, she put out her hands towards him. 'Truly—I'm so sorry . . . I didn't mean to do that.'

He said tersely, 'You must go away at once. You may take the fever. You should have known better than to touch him. It could be contagious.'

He pushed her to one side, and went to the bed.

'Etienne . . .' he called softly. 'Etienne! Do you know me? It is Guy Dupré . . .'

The fevered man moaned and tossed, and Dupré straightened up, an expression of resignation on his face.

Mariana, who had been watching him closely, said soberly, 'It is because of him that you have halted here.'

'I will not abandon him,' he replied harshly, 'or any others who are wounded. I will abandon no man in Spain, if I can possibly get him home to France.'

Home. It all fell into place. These men did not seek Felipe. The French no longer had the time or cause to fight that furtive and cruel war. These dragoons had been recalled to France to defend their own land against the advancing British. Other things she had heard him say, but to which she had attached insufficient significance, bore this out.

Her mind in a whirl, she thought: How many men are the French withdrawing like this? And how could she get word of her discovery to Felipe?

Her attention was drawn back to the sick man, and Felipe receded into the background, of lesser importance.

'You must fetch a doctor for him,' she urged. 'I know of one.'

'Doctors don't come to fever patients. Besides, he needs no doctor.'

'Does not need one?' she cried. 'How can you say such a thing?'

'He is dying!' he returned angrily. 'What would a physician do, but dose him with some foul concoction which would make him more wretched? Let him die quietly! At least he will not fall into the hands of your friends in the hills.'

'Fel—', Mariana checked herself just in time. '*They* would not harm a dying man,' she protested.

'Are you really so innocent? Captured wounded or sick French stragglers have been thrown alive into fires such as I saw burn on the skyline last night!' he replied brutally. 'They would like nothing better than to get their hands on him.'

Mariana flushed and felt sick. She had heard such stories but always blocked her mind to them, even if she could not block her ears, telling herself that Felipe, at least, would never commit such a crime against humanity.

'Then send for a priest if he is dying!' she begged desperately. 'You cannot refuse him that!'

'A priest?' he exclaimed. He glanced at the bed.

'No man can help Lieutenant Legrand now,' he said at last, abruptly. 'He will have to make his own peace with God.'

He turned away from the bed and, going across to the window, threw back the other half of the shutters, revealing a dramatic and beautiful vista of the distant Pyrenees. For a moment he stood there, staring out intently, almost as if he would see beyond the mountains, to France. Then he sat down heavily on the long seat in the window embrasure and leaned his head back against the wall.

'This is an accursed country for us,' he said, more to himself than to her. 'Beautiful and cruel, demanding some sacrifice, some price which must be paid in blood. I think that, for you Spaniards, blood and death take the place of love.'

'You should have reckoned with that before you invaded our country,' Mariana retorted proudly. 'You have been taught a long overdue lesson here in Spain, you Frenchmen! The whole of Europe does *not* belong to your Emperor. We Spaniards have not allowed you to trample upon us as you have done upon the other nations whose borders you have violated, villages burned and way of life destroyed!'

For a moment he stared at her, as if surprised at her outburst. Then a faint flush darkened his prominent cheekbones beneath the bronzed skin, and she saw a glint in his eyes. Mariana began to fear she had been unwise to antagonise him by pouring out her feelings so freely. She was, after all, this man's prisoner.

'What do you know of it?' he said savagely. 'I have seen your *guerra al cuchillo*—your war to the knife! I call it murder. Tell me, señorita—your lover out there in the hills, how many men have died at his hands? Not killed in the heat of battle, mind you, but in cold blood and by stealth, in the darkness. A knife slipped between the ribs gently . . . so.' He gestured with his hand, illustrating his words. Seeing her turn pale, he added sarcastically, 'Doesn't he boast to you of his exploits? His successes? Next time you're in his bed, ask him!'

'I have no lover in the hills,' Mariana said tightly.

He gave an exclamation of disgust. 'Pah! You pious little hypocrite! *You* wanted to fetch a priest to Etienne Legrand? Go and light a candle to whichever plaster saint protects you, and next time you're confessing your sins, spare a thought for the men your friends have butchered with the knife, burned or hacked into pieces alive, hung up on trees, and dispatched in a dozen ways more satanic than any invention of a medieval hell!'

'I won't believe it!' Mariana cried. 'At least, not of—not of all of them!'

'So he's not only a lover, but a hero, too!' he returned mockingly. 'I'm growing curious to meet this modern El Cid!' He leaned his head back against the wall again, and stared at her thoughtfully beneath half-lowered eyelids. 'Come here.'

'W-what?' Mariana stepped back in alarm.

'You heard me well enough. Come here!' He

pointed to the place on the window-seat beside him.

'I'd prefer not to,' Mariana stammered.

'I'm not interested in what you prefer. I give the orders here.' He snapped his fingers. 'I said, sit down there!' His voice cracked sharply, with the force of a pistol-shot.

Mariana walked unwillingly towards him and sat down as far away from him as possible, pressing back against the wall, but still all too close to the aggressive masculinity of his dishevelled and battle-scarred appearance. There was a look in his eye she did not like, and feared, because she had seen it in a man's face before. She had seen it in Felipe's, sometimes, when he looked at her, and she knew what it meant.

But if, in Felipe's eyes, that look had always frightened her, in this man's it also caused a strange stirring of her emotions, and filled her with a curious sense of unease, as though, deep within herself, she was unsure of herself. Something of this must have shown in her face, because he smiled slightly. It was not a smile which encouraged her.

'What do you think I might do?' he asked in a tone of quiet, almost casual, insolence. 'Do you think I might give your Patriotic Hero some cause for jealousy?'

He reached out his hand lazily and gave a tug to the loosely knotted silk shawl. The knot unravelled, and the shawl slid softly from her shoulders with a faint rustle, revealing the near-nakedness of the thin cotton chemise.

'I will say one thing for our friend in the hills,' he remarked. 'He has excellent taste in women.'

'If you were not already wounded,' Mariana managed to say with difficulty. 'I would slap your face.'

'Why don't you slap it anyway?' he taunted her. 'Perhaps you don't really want to? Or are you squeamish? It puts you off, this?' He pointed to his scarred face, and gave a twisted grin. 'I can't believe you're sorry for me.'

'Sorry? For you?' she exclaimed incredulously. 'You are a—a coarse, arrogant, conceited ruffian! No better than a bandit. Any Spanish peasant would have better manners than you!'

Before any other man she would have betrayed the shame she felt at her scanty clothing. But, though miserably aware that the inadequate chemise accentuated, rather than disguised, the soft contours of her young body, she would not allow this man the satisfaction of seeing he had humiliated her. She tossed back her chestnut hair, and stared at him defiantly.

'Oh, I can be very pleasant,' he said softly, 'in the right circumstances. Why don't you try me, mmn?' He wound his fingers in a lock of her hair. 'I think you'll find me as good as our friend in the hills—perhaps better, who knows?'

His grip on her hair tightened as he made to draw her towards him.

Mariana gave a gasp and wrenched her hair from his grasp, at the same time sending her hand swinging towards the unscarred side of his face.

But he was too quick, and seized her wrist, holding her arm, upraised to strike him, but powerless.

'Ah—ah!' he said reproachfully. 'That was foolish.'

'Let go of me!' she gasped, trying to free herself.

'Why should I? Tell me that,' he countered. 'Who's going to come running to save you, if you scream? That devoted maid of yours? I'll tell Beaudoin to lock her up. Perhaps the British have us retreating, but you are still part of the spoils of war, *querida*. Tell me why I shouldn't enjoy them while they are still mine to take!'

'No!' Mariana somehow twisted her wrist free and put both hands against his chest, pushing him away from her. 'You won't—I won't let you!'

'Won't *let*?' He smiled his lop-sided grin. 'Even given my damaged state, you couldn't stop me, not if I really wanted to . . .'

She looked at him wildly, her mouth parted to speak, but unable to force the words past her frozen lips.

Suddenly he stood up and tossed the silk shawl contemptuously into her lap.

'But a pleasure shared is a pleasure doubled,' he said. 'I'll wait for you to change your mind!'

Mariana snatched at the shawl and pulled it hastily round her bare shoulders as she scrambled to her feet.

'You will wait for ever! I'll never change my mind on that!' she promised him angrily.

He hunched his shoulders in a peculiarly Gallic manner. 'Women always say that. They like to be cajoled, begged. They surrender fast enough in the end. Once you've made sufficient play of defending your virtue, I won't even have to ask . . .'

Mariana drew in her breath with a gasp. 'You are unspeakable!' she hissed. 'You lack even the elements of common decency. Not only have you no respect for me, you do not even respect the presence of your dying comrade over there! You are beneath contempt!'

He paled and she thought for a moment he would fly into a rage. Then he said in a low, hard voice: 'Your opinion of me is of no importance, señorita. What matters is that while you are in this house you obey my orders and don't make a nuisance of yourself. There will be no more wandering about in this haphazard fashion, interfering in matters which do not concern you. Is that understood?'

Mariana flushed and turned away with a swirl of her petticoat. The sick man stirred, tossing restlessly on his pillows, and she went to the bedside and took up the damp towel again to wipe his forehead gently. Her hand was shaking, not because she was afraid of the fever, but because her emotions were in a turmoil.

Guy Dupré had gone to the door. 'I told you to leave him alone.'

'I would prefer to stay with him,' Mariana said in a steady tone. 'Someone must.'

'Permission refused!' he returned sharply. 'Go back to your own room.'

There was a small ebony and silver crucifix on the wall by the bed. Mariana lifted it down and tucked it into the sick man's fingers. It seemed to her he gripped it, but perhaps it was only a reflex action. She turned away and her eyes met those of Guy Dupré, standing in the doorway of the room, one hand raised above his head and holding the lintel.

'It is very hot in this house,' she said in a low voice, 'and it is our custom to take the air in the evenings, when it is cool. Have I your *permission* to walk in the garden later, with my maid? I won't try and run away!' she added with asperity. 'I give you my word—on the honour of my family.'

'Ah, that Spanish honour,' he said drily. 'Very well. But don't go far. You see that little grove of orange-trees down there?' He nodded towards the open window. 'You may go as far as that, but no further.'

'Thank you,' Mariana said stiffly. She had not really expected him to agree.

'Did you misunderstand my earlier instructions?' he asked brusquely. 'I said, change the gown—not take it off and wander about half naked. Cover yourself up!'

'I understand you perfectly!' Mariana told him evenly.

But as she passed him in the narrow doorway, he caught at her arm roughly, restraining her.

'Remember what I said about keeping away from my men!' he said in a cold voice. 'Almost all of them have known comrades mutilated and murdered by your friends in the hills. They have no love for any Spaniard, man or woman!' He released her and watched her walk away.

CHAPTER
FOUR

IT WAS cool in the gardens, and agreeable to the
eye, but Mariana was in no mood to take any
pleasure in her surroundings. Juana, enveloped in a
black shawl, walked beside her on the gravel path,
chattering, with hardly a pause for breath, of all she
had observed in the kitchens and of the liberties
taken by the occupiers with the ducal plate and
linen. Her voice flowed over Mariana, who heard it
as if it came muffled and from a distance, through a
blanketing fog of her own thoughts.

This was not the first time she had encountered
the French. They had been in Spain in force since
1808, after all. But it was the first time she had been
obliged to meet closely with any of the fighting
units of the line. Previously their French 'visitors'
had taken the form of parties of the so-called
Gendarmerie of Spain, a familiar enough sight in
their blue coats and cocked hats. In their efforts to
hunt out the guerrilla bands and guarantee safe
passage for French couriers on the highroads, these
gentlemen had made fairly regular appearances in
the neighbourhood. On one occasion they had
stayed a week in the village. Mariana had found
them surly, suspicious and ill-tempered—but well

disciplined, respecting civilian life and property.

These dragoons were another matter altogether. No other section of the Grand Army had earned itself such a reputation for ruthless brutality. The appearance of dragoons in any village was received with fear and dread, and to them were attributed many of the atrocities which had lit the fires of revenge in the hearts of the Spanish peasantry.

These, then, were the men with whom she was trapped. She was the prisoner of their leader, a man she regarded as an armed and uniformed plunderer, all the more dangerous for being a part of a defeated and retreating army, just as the lion when wounded is the more to be feared. To make matters worse, she suspected he was a womaniser, bound by no code of chivalry and, despite his insolent offer to 'wait', unaccustomed to brook refusal. Mariana had no experience to help her to understand the pattern of such a man's thinking. He frightened her, and he fascinated her, too, to be honest. It was as if he offered her a challenge which she feared and hated, but in some strange and inexplicable way longed to accept.

Mariana burst out fiercely now: 'The French pride themselves on being a civilised nation! They like to talk of culture and of love. In fact they care nothing for the weak or the dying, and believe themselves entitled to make their odious advances to any woman they please! Felipe told me they were all libertines, and now I can see for myself he was right!'

'They say,' said Juana with a certain relish, 'that

King Joseph had so many loose women in his entourage that it was as if he travelled with his own private brothel.'

'I shouldn't be at all surprised,' said Mariana moodily.

They had reached the stone basin of a fountain. In the centre, Neptune rose from the waves in his stone chariot, horses snorting and flailing webbed feet instead of hooves. Alas, the poor monarch no longer ruled the waves, for the stone basin was quite dry and partly filled with dust and leaves.

'Just like poor Joseph Bonaparte,' Mariana said. 'He wanted to rule Spain, and it all turned to dust.'

They walked on until they reached the edge of the orange-grove. The red-gold fruits had long been picked, but the stubby little trees linked their neglected and unpruned branches so that the thick foliage formed a solid screen of dark, bitter green. Unfriendly, almost sinister, they seemed to ward off the inquisitive stranger. Within the grove all was quiet, dark and still.

'I promised I would go no further,' Mariana said with a sigh, stopping before the first line of trees. 'I suppose we must go back. I hate the idea of returning to that house, but I gave my word.' She turned.

There was a faint rustle behind them, and they both gasped, startled and alarmed, as a man materialised with total unexpectedness from among the dark green leaves.

Mariana gave a cry. 'Felipe!'

'God bless you, Don Felipe!' Juana exclaimed, bursting into tears. 'You've come to rescue my lady.'

Felipe motioned her urgently to keep her voice down, and whispered, 'Go and keep watch!'

Juana obediently scuttled back down the path to the stone fountain, and sat down on the rim, whence she had a good view of the back of the house.

'You are quite safe? They have not harmed you?' Felipe demanded, catching at Mariana's hand. 'Tell me!'

'No, no!' she assured him, fearing his hot temper. 'I'm quite all right. But, Felipe, you shouldn't have come. It's madness! Captain Dupré believes I met someone up in the hills last night. As yet, thank goodness, he doesn't realise it was the White Wolf. If he knew, he would kill me. He spoke of the White Wolf with such hatred, Felipe. I couldn't describe it to you.'

'Let him hate me,' Felipe said, in an amused voice. A slight smile touched the corners of his mouth. 'He won't catch me!'

'Don't be so sure!' Mariana warned him. 'He's a very clever man. He knows whoever it was I met may try to rescue me, and they are certainly patrolling these gardens. Felipe, you must go at once. But there is one thing you must know first.' She caught at his sleeve. 'These men have not come especially to hunt for you. They are on their way home to France.'

'To France? Are you sure?' He frowned. 'Do you

mean, they have been ordered back?'

'Yes, yes! Don't you see what it means? The Spanish war really is over!'

'Oh, I understand what it means,' he told her softly. 'But as to whether they will reach France, that is another matter.'

There was an odd pause in which the garden suddenly seemed a very still place. Even the birds, singing their evening lullabies in the branches, had fallen silent.

'I thought that we wished them to leave Spain,' Mariana said at last. 'That is what we have fought for these past five years.'

'And we still fight!' he said sharply, a fierce gleam in his dark eyes. 'We did not ask them to invade our country, and they will not leave Spain so easily as they entered it!' His voice sank to a hiss. 'And where they remain, *I* shall find them. I shall not leave those hills while one French soldier remains on Spanish soil. He is my enemy, and I shall never let him escape!'

An icy chill ran up Mariana's spine and laid cold fingers on her heart. She withdrew her hand from his, but he caught at her wrist.

'Come quickly!' he urged her, pulling her forward. 'No one will see us if we go this way. Juana will stay where she is and make as if talking to someone. It will be a little while before they come to look for you.'

'But I can't, Felipe,' she faltered, hanging back. 'I gave my word. Where could I go, in any case? I can't go home. They'll find me.'

'You will come to the hills, with me,' he returned, impatiently.

'No!' Mariana almost shouted the word, starting back and staring at him wildly.

She had lived in the constant dread that one day he would ask her to join him in the guerrilla camp. Not only patriotism had spurred her to act as his courier and informant, his eyes and ears. She had wanted him to see how useful it was to have her in the village, so that he would leave her there, in comparative peace. But she had always known that if ever the day came that her position in the village was jeopardised, or she could no longer be of help to him there, then he would suggest she join him. It had been a recurring nightmare.

He was looking at her now, his eyebrows raised questioningly, struck by the force of her refusal.

Nervously, she began to babble excuses. 'I would be a hindrance to you, Felipe, slow you down, complicate your decisions. You've always said that women have no place in the guerrilla bands.'

'It's true I've never allowed women to join us. I can't be encumbered with a raggle-taggle of women and children. But this is different! You can't stay here, among these men. It will be a hard life in the hills, but you will be safe—and we shall be together,' he added in a low voice.

'Don Felipe!' Juana called. 'Make haste—someone's coming!'

'They'll find you!' Mariana exclaimed, pushing him towards the orange-grove. 'Quickly, Felipe! It doesn't matter about me. The important thing is that they don't capture the White Wolf! I'll stay here and distract them, only go!'

He hesitated briefly, glancing towards Juana who was gesticulating frantically.

'Very well,' he said, 'but I'll come back. Try and come here again!' He squeezed her arm in hasty farewell and with a faint crackle of dry twigs he was gone, a shadow among the trees.

Seconds later, Michel Boucher burst into view and came to a halt, staring aggressively at Mariana.

'Where is he?' he demanded hoarsely. 'You speak French, the sergeant said so—so speak up now!'

'Where is who?' Mariana retaliated coldly, angered at being addressed in so disrespectful a manner.

'Don't play games with me!' Boucher snarled. 'Captain Dupré said I was to watch out for you, just in case! He's not sure whether you're in league with those devils in the hills—but I've got no doubts! You were talking to a man just now. I heard his voice.'

'You are quite stupid,' Mariana told him disdainfully. 'I was talking to my maid.'

'Were you, now?' he returned sarcastically. 'We'll see about that!'

He unslung his carbine and pushed roughly past her into the orange-grove.

Mariana and Juana exchanged nervous glances, but at that moment there came the unexpected sound of shots and shouting voices from near to the house. Mariana's expression turned to one of alarm, and Boucher burst out of the grove and set off back towards the house as if he had a whole squadron of enemy cavalry at his heels.

'Dear Lord!' wailed Juana, crossing herself rapidly. 'Those devils have spotted Don Felipe and are shooting at him. They'll kill him, for sure!'

'Be quiet! We don't know that,' urged Mariana. 'Stay here!'

But afraid that the maid was right, she picked up her skirts in both hands and ran after Boucher, towards the house, as Juana called after her despairingly.

Seen from the gardens, the house appeared upon a raised terrace, bordered by a stone balustrade. A flight of steps led up from the lower level of the gardens. As Mariana reached it, she could see that Guy stood on the terrace by the open window of his room, out of which he had apparently just climbed. The burly figure of Beaudoin was crouched incongruously behind a statue of Diana the Huntress. He was signalling frantically to someone she could not see, and Boucher was racing like a hare towards the stable block, brandishing his carbine.

'What's happening?' Mariana cried out, running up the steps. 'Why are you shooting—'

'For God's sake,' Dupré shouted, 'get down!'

Then several things happened at once. As he spoke, the captain launched himself towards her and, seizing her by the arm, dragged her behind the shelter of a large stone urn. At the same moment there was a crack, and a bullet sped across the open space where Mariana had stood a split second

before, and struck part of the balustrade, sending
stone chips flying in all directions, before ricochet-
ing through a window.

'How many men?' yelled Dupré to Beaudoin
above the sound of crashing glass, clasping Mariana
to his chest so tightly that she could hardly breathe.

'Only one man, Captain, over by the stables. I
can see him!' Beaudoin called.

'Felipe!' thought Mariana in despair, as she
pressed her face into the captain's coat. 'It is
Felipe!'

There was another shot, followed by some shouting, and then silence. Boucher and another trooper
came back towards the house, and Beaudoin
emerged from behind the statue to converse with
them. Boucher pointed behind him, beyond the
stables.

'You saved my life,' Mariana said soberly to Guy
Dupré, trying to extricate herself from his arms
with dignity.

He seemed to recollect he held her fast in his
embrace and, releasing her, said curtly, 'You nearly cost me mine! Haven't you any sense? Whatever
made you run out across open ground like that
while bullets were flying about? Another time,
have the wit to get behind something, or down on
the ground!' He turned to Beaudoin, who had
come up to them. 'Well?'

'He got away, sir,' said Beaudoin apologetically.
'But some of the men got a good look at him. It was
that rascally muleteer. He's been hanging about the
place ever since we came.'

'Paco!' Mariana exclaimed, her relief echoing in her voice. 'It was Paco you saw!'

Both men looked at her.

'I mean, I know him,' she added hastily to Guy. 'Everyone knows him. He's a local man. He only wanted to get his mules back. They're his livelihood. I'm so glad you didn't kill him.'

'He was firing at us!' he replied crisply. 'For my part, I'm anything but pleased to hear my men let him escape.' To Beaudoin, he added in French, 'Double the guard on those mules. We need them.'

As Beaudoin went off, Guy turned back to Mariana and asked very quietly, but in a voice which brooked no nonsense, 'And now, señorita, you can tell me whom you thought it was, before you discovered it was the muleteer.'

'I didn't know who it was! But I can understand what Paco was doing there. You stole those mules from him!'

'Come inside,' he said grimly. 'You and I are going to have a little talk.'

With a sinking heart, Mariana followed him into the house. In his room, she faced him defiantly and declared, more to convince herself than him, 'I am not afraid of you!'

'Sit down, Mariana, here.' With one hand he dragged out a chair in a token gesture of courtesy, and went to seat himself on the window-sill, whence he could see his men searching the outbuildings for the muleteer.

He looked drawn, and there were little beads of sweat on his forehead and temples. Mariana realised that the violent lunge he had made to save her had probably reopened the partly healed wound in his side. Even as this thought entered her head, he slipped his hand under his coat, wincing.

'Why should you be afraid, if you tell the truth?' he demanded tersely. 'The truth is what I want, Mariana. So far you've told me nothing, and I'm not in the mood to be patient, or to be fed lies! I am under orders to get back across the Pyrenees. I am responsible for those men out there. There is a sniper somewhere taking pot-shots at us. Your friends in the hills are awaiting their chance. I have sick and wounded. Etienne Legrand is dying upstairs, and my ribs hurt like hell!'

'I'm sorry . . .' Mariana ventured.

'Sorry! *Sorry?* Do you think I give a damn whether or not you are sorry?' he shouted at her. He drew a deep breath and pointed a finger at her menacingly. 'Don't play foolish games with me, Mariana!'

Mariana bit her lips nervously. She did not doubt that the implied threat was real. Not only Felipe's safety, but her own future, depended on what she said now. To invent some wild tale would be useless. He would know at once. Besides which, she did not want to lie unnecessarily to him. It would be a miserable and ignoble thing to do to a man who had just saved her life at some risk to his own. His action had aggravated his injuries and she could not but feel responsible. To see him in pain distressed her. Despite everything, she wanted to go and help him, but her help would hardly be welcome.

'I have to go back a little, if you are to understand,' she said hesitantly.

'Go on!' he said curtly.

'I'll tell you as best I can.' She folded her hands in her lap and took a deep breath. 'I had a brother— only the one—and he died fighting in our Spanish army, at Ocaña.'

He fixed her with a keen look and nodded. 'I know it. I was there. The Spanish generals were fools to fight on such ground. If it was a massacre; it was not the fault of the French, it was the fault of those who led your brother and others to their deaths. I'm sorry for your loss, but other men died that day, too.'

'Does that make the loss of any one man less painful?' Mariana demanded bitterly.

'And how many men do you think I've seen die?' he retaliated. 'Bury your dead, and forget them.'

'Forget? Forget what? That I am Spanish, or that my brother was a Spaniard?' Mariana cried out impetuously. 'He was the last son of an old and respected house! He died defending his own land, his own people! Tell me, Captain, should I forget that?'

'I do not require to be taught the elements of patriotism by a woman!' he said harshly. 'Leave the heroic speeches to your menfolk!'

'I am the last of my family,' Mariana said in a low voice which shook slightly. 'It speaks through me, or it is silent for ever.'

He raised his head and stared at her slight, rigid figure and pale face in which her large hazel eyes, fringed with dark lashes, were fixed on his, and she thought she saw him flush.

He lifted his hand in a placatory gesture and said tersely, but much more quietly, 'Go on!'

'After Ocaña,' Mariana said soberly, 'many of our soldiers lost heart . . .'

Felipe's voice echoed in her head from that terrible time—*We shall no longer be fodder for the French guns! We shall fight on from the hills, where Napoleon's cannon will be useless, and the advantage will be ours!*

Aloud, she said, 'My brother had a very close friend. He—he is out there, in the hills, hiding . . .' She pointed through the open window.

'You mean, he is a deserter!' he interrupted sarcastically.

She had been so afraid to lie to him, and now it seemed she did not need to. She had only to tell him enough of the truth—and no more—to lead him to form a conclusion for himself, one which was logical but inaccurate. A simple deserter on the run was real enough to be believed, and he was no White Wolf. She saw the captain's expression clear. For a moment, he almost looked relieved.

'He was Miguel's friend . . .' she explained truthfully.

'And now he is your lover? He's made progress, your deserter! How would Miguel have viewed that?'

'He is not my lover!' Mariana denied with unfeigned emotion. 'I am the last survivor of an ancient family! My father was *alcalde* here in this district. Do you think I have the cheap morals of a camp follower?'

Guy stirred slightly, shifting his weight on the window-sill. She expected him to return some biting reply but, to her surprise, he only nodded and then leaned his head back, closing his eyes.

Disconcerted, Mariana asked hesitantly, 'Are you all right?' Her ear caught the involuntary note of anxiety in her voice.

'I'm all right!' he said sharply, but still without opening his eyes. 'Go on!'

'I take this man food,' she said simply. 'When your men captured me, I had taken him food as I always do. I had only just left him, and I thought they would go after him and capture him, and kill him. So I didn't say anything to them—not that they gave me any chance!' she added pointedly.

'And you thought that might have been he, out there, just now, blasting away at anything that moved?'

'I could not be sure it wasn't! He's a Spaniard, hot-headed and impetuous. But it wasn't he, it was only poor Paco, who really is not very bright and can't be blamed for behaving as he did. I'm just so relieved you didn't kill him, and he didn't kill any of your men.'

'You could have told me this earlier, this morning!' he said.

'You were so angry, you kept talking about the White Wolf. Captain Dupré, please,' Mariana said entreatingly, 'how could I tell you any of this before?'

He grunted, and after a moment or two opened his eyes and muttered, 'It's only half a story!' He left his window to walk to the desk in the centre of the room, and move some sheets of paper around at random, apparently as an aid to thought. 'Is there a washerwoman in the village?' he asked suddenly.

Mariana gaped at him. 'A—a what?'

'A washerwoman!' he repeated impatiently. 'All my shirts are ready to fall off my back with grime and sweat.'

'There are women who take washing to the public fountain,' Mariana faltered. 'Or you could give your linen to Juana, my maid. She would probably agree to do it for you, if I asked her.'

'I'll pay her,' he said, in a businesslike manner.

Mariana frowned. Did all this mean he had accepted her story, or not? Perhaps he wanted time to think it over, to seek out some flaw in it.

'Shall I ask Juana then?' she ventured.

'Yes, yes, go on . . .' He gestured towards the door in a brusque dismissal of her presence, shrugging off his green coat as he did so.

'There's nothing else?' she persisted.

'You should know that better than I!' he said sourly. 'I told you I'd finished with you for now.'

Mariana got up hesitantly and went towards the door. As she stretched out her hand towards the handle, the coat was flung to the floor and there was a slight clatter. She turned.

He had thrown himself down on the camp-bed in the corner, on his back, one arm folded across his face. The other hand was clasped to his side.

Mariana ran back across the room and dropped on her knees by him.

'Let me see that,' she said gently, and, without waiting for a reply, took his hand away from his side. His palm was smeared with fresh blood, and a new red stain was soaking through the linen of his shirt.

'Can you sit up?' she asked. 'That needs a new dressing.'

'No bandages,' he muttered. 'Leave it alone. It will congeal by itself.'

'Don't talk such rubbish!' she said crossly. She hesitated, then stood up and walked a few steps away. 'Close your eyes!' she ordered, and stooping, grasped the cotton flounce of her petticoat firmly and with a determined jerk ripped it away. The stitching broke easily and she was left with a slightly ornate, but perfectly serviceable, bandage in her hand.

'To have a young lady—the *alcalde*'s daughter, no less—sacrificing her petticoat for me, is an honour indeed,' he said faintly from the bed. 'But I don't know why I have to close my eyes. You were walking around in that petticoat and very little else, earlier.'

'If you had any kind of manners, you would have forgotten that,' Mariana muttered resentfully.

'My ribs are cracked, not my brain!' he retorted. He pushed himself upright to sit on the edge of the camp-bed and allowed her to divest him of his shirt.

'Ugh!' Mariana muttered at the messy clotted bandage this process revealed.

'The damn thing's opened up,' Guy said irritably, craning his neck to peer at the injury. 'Get out of my light, can't you? Go and get Beaudoin, if you want to do something useful.'

'He's outside. I can't fetch him. Keep still, I can do it. I only need some water.' Mariana went to inspect the washbasin. 'This will have to do.'

Gingerly she managed to unwind the old bandages. The wound itself ran for about seven inches diagonally across his ribs, surrounded by an area of purple skin. It had begun to knit together, but now seeped blood angrily.

'Should it be that colour?' Mariana asked.

'It's not infected,' he replied impatiently. 'I kept washing it with brandy. That did the trick. If you're going to turn faint on me, leave it alone!'

'You don't have to be so rude!' she flared at him.

'Get on with it, then,' he grumbled.

Mariana picked up the new bandage and leaned towards him. Her long chestnut hair brushed against his bare chest as she stretched her arm round behind him with the bandage. A little nervously, she fumbled with the cotton strip, almost dropping it, and as she retrieved it her cheek pressed briefly against his collarbone. His skin was warm, damp and sticky, and clung to hers. She could feel the rapid beating of his heart against her own breast.

Suddenly his hand gripped her shoulder painfully. Mariana gave a startled cry, and looked up into his eyes to see that they shone with an odd, disquieting light.

'I said, go and get Beaudoin!' he said hoarsely. His face was flushed and he was breathing heavily. 'Go on!' He pushed her away so roughly that she lost her balance and sprawled inelegantly on the floor at his feet.

Mariana scrambled up, frightened and bewildered, not knowing what had suddenly led him to this violence.

'But I can—' she began.

'Damn you, why can you do nothing I ask of you!' he rasped, lurching to his feet and towards the open window. 'Sergeant!' he yelled through it into the garden. He twisted to face her, his features contorted. 'Get out of here!' He drew a choking breath. '*Get out!*'

He moved towards her, so much fury in his expression that Mariana turned and ran blindly from the room in a panic.

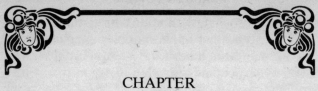

CHAPTER
FIVE

She had succeeded in allaying the captain's suspicions, at least for the time being, even if his injury and his temper appeared both to have been aggravated by the episode on the terrace. But Felipe had said he would come back—and Felipe was a man of his word. Somehow, Guy Dupré must be persuaded to release her, and to that end she was obliged to seek an interview with him again, however much her heart sank at the prospect.

Mariana turned now before the long glass in the painted bedroom, studying the effect of a rose silk gown with long, tight sleeves. A muslin fichu round the neck and across the low-cut bosom of the gown effectively disguised the décolleté. The result was suitably modest and demure. Captain Dupré could hardly object.

She had rejected three or four gowns before settling on this one. Despite everything, Mariana had to admit to a certain pleasure in trying on the absent Duchess's wardrobe. At first she had felt a slight embarrassment at making free with someone else's clothes, but then she had thought that the absentee could hardly have set any store by these dresses, or she would have taken them with her to

Madrid. Also, latest rumour had it, the Duchess had fled with other Spanish nobles who had taken service with King Joseph and was now safely across the Pyrenees, in France.

Juana had dressed Mariana's hair in a curly topknot, and Mariana picked up the tortoiseshell comb and fixed it carefully to secure the chestnut swirl. Her complexion was wan, and she pinched her cheeks vigorously, and painfully, to bring up a pink colour.

If she was pale, it was because she had slept badly. The rain had begun during the night, a heavy downpour accompanied by thunder which had threatened all the previous day. Towards dawn it had turned to a steady drizzle which promised to continue throughout the morning. Through the streaked window-panes she could see the gardens, glistening and damp. A heavy mist obscured the distant Pyrenees; even the nearer hills were lost to view. An odd sense of relief lightened her heart when she saw this, as if the mist held Felipe a prisoner, over there on the rain-soaked hillsides, and kept him from making contact with her.

Lying awake last night, listening to the rain beating on the shutters, she had sought a way out of her predicament as fruitlessly as any poor caged mouse running round and round his tiny prison. She was truly between the devil and the deep blue sea—between a man who claimed to love her, but the very touch of whose hand she dreaded, and this terrifying Frenchman who might yet decide to have her shot, and yet who fascinated her.

To hate the French, who had taken Miguel from her, had always been so simple. Now 'the French' were represented in the one person of Guy Dupré, and she no longer felt certain what name to give the emotion she felt. But she had already once glimpsed in his eyes that look which saw her not as a prisoner, but as a woman, and if she stayed here very long, sooner or later she would see that look again.

As all these thoughts had drifted through her tormented brain, she had fancied she heard the captain's voice, quite near at hand, and had sat up in bed, listening intently, the bedclothes drawn tightly about her in apprehension. At one time, she was almost sure she heard the clatter of feet descending the marble staircase. But afterwards, though she had strained her ears, they had caught nothing but the staccato rattle of the rain and the growl of the departing thunder. Perhaps it had been only her imagination. He haunted it. It was as if he stood always by her. She began to fear she would never be free of him. No matter what happened to any of them, this Frenchman would never leave her mind.

Resolutely, Mariana thrust these uncomfortable thoughts from her and turned from the looking-glass. She went out into the corridor and glanced along it. To her surprise, the door to Lieutenant Legrand's room stood ajar, and an unusual silence hung over the house.

Filled with some foreboding, Mariana went quietly to the door of the sick-room and pushed it open. The bed was empty. The bedclothes lay in a rumpled heap on the floor, and the lower sheet had been stripped from the mattress and was missing.

Mariana turned and ran wildly down the great staircase, calling loudly, 'Captain Dupré! Captain Dupré!'

She wrenched frantically at the door of his room and flung it open. It, too, was empty, though his belongings were still there. The noise of a footstep behind her caused her to whirl round.

'He's busy,' Beaudoin said, his solid frame filling the doorway.

'Where is he?' Mariana demanded in agitation. 'And where is the sick lieutenant? I went into his room and the bed is empty. I thought you'd all gone! Where is everyone?'

Beaudoin glanced towards the rain-soaked windows. 'Some over at the stables, some out with the burial party.'

'The lieutenant . . . ?' Mariana whispered. 'Oh, no . . .' She sat down heavily on the nearest chair. 'I was trying on dresses,' she said to herself dully, in Spanish. 'I was trying on dresses, and that poor young man was lying dead in the next room.'

'What's that?' Beaudoin asked.

'Nothing,' she said sadly in French. 'I was only thinking . . . about the poor lieutenant. I could have sat with him. He needn't have died alone.' (And I would have stayed with him, she thought in growing anger, had I been allowed to do so.)

Beaudoin was staring at her thoughtfully, his

weathered, battered features looking as if they had been carved from a piece of pink granite.

'He wasn't alone,' he said at last. 'The captain sat up with him all night, right until early this morning, when he died.'

'That must have been when I heard his voice,' Mariana recalled soberly.

She had been wrong to accuse him of callousness towards the dying man. He had been there all night, a wall's thickness away, watching, and waiting, keeping a lonely vigil.

Beaudoin gave her a shrewd look. 'Don't upset yourself, mademoiselle, the lieutentant's better dead. We couldn't have taken him along with us, and we couldn't have left him behind for those other fellows . . .' He nodded towards the windows and the unseen, mist-obscured, hills.

Those other fellows. It was Beaudoin who had originally thought her a spy and brought her to this house, a prisoner. Had he deliberately reminded her of the *guerrilleros* who waited, like vultures, around a weakened foe?

She looked up and saw he was still watching her, scowling.

'What do you want him for?' he demanded gruffly.

'Want him for?' She stared at Beaudoin a little foolishly.

'Captain Dupré, why do you want him?' Beaudoin repeated doggedly.

'I—I wanted to ask him about me, about what he means to do with me.'

Beaudoin came a little further into the room, a burly, forthright figure, solid as a rock.

'*I* brought you here,' he said in a despondent tone which would have seemed almost comical had it not been so sincere. 'That was my mistake. I shouldn't have done it.'

'What do you mean?' Mariana, puzzled, searched his face which, with its full drooping moustaches and lugubrious expression, had the look of a mournful walrus.

Beaudoin said obstinately, 'I shouldn't have brought you here. He's got enough to worry him. He doesn't need you.'

'If Captain Dupré had released me that first night,' Mariana replied angrily, 'I'd be no worry to anyone!' Not even to myself, she thought.

'He's a good officer, and a good man,' Beaudoin continued in his dogged way. 'This—' Beaudoin tapped his own barrel-like ribs, 'gives him more trouble than he'll ever admit. *I* know. He has enough to worry about now, without woman trouble. That's the last thing he needs.'

'Meaning me?' Mariana demanded icily.

'Meaning you,' Beaudoin answered bluntly.

'I want nothing from your Captain Dupré!' Mariana told him strongly. 'I was brought here against my will, and kept here a prisoner. I can't help your captain's troubles. If he chooses to make more for himself, it's not my doing.'

'Women!' muttered Beaudoin scornfully, the supreme misogynist. 'They don't have to *do* anything. Just by being there, one of them can cause a man more trouble than a dozen generals can make for him.'

He turned and stomped morosely out of the room, letting the door crash behind him.

Mariana was left alone, seething with resentment. She did not blame loyal Beaudoin for his misplaced honesty. She blamed Guy Dupré. All this, everything, was his fault. She glanced at the rain-streaked window. Somewhere, out there, Guy would be assisting at the burial of his comrade. Papers covered the surface of his desk, and any one of them might contain information of vital interest to the Spanish–British cause. She might never have another such opportunity.

Mariana went hastily to the desk and began to search feverishly. Casualty lists, fodder requirements, some memorandum about the lack of suitable remounts—and a single sheet of paper pushed away underneath all the others. Mariana snatched it up.

It was a partly written private letter. She compared the handwriting with that on the other sheets. Yes, this was his—neat, elegant, the lines level, the 'd's' with identical curly tops to them. The hand of an educated man, and one to whom legibility was important.

'Those law studies,' Mariana muttered, 'left their mark.'

She sat down in his chair and, frowning in concentration, began to read.

'My dearest Lisette,' the letter began.

Lisette? Mariana's brow puckered and she read

on with even closer attention.

'I have recently received—you can imagine, if you will, with what pleasure—your last two letters, which arrived together, the one having taken four, and the other three, months to find me. I have read and re-read them till they threaten to disintegrate into mere shreds. To have news of you, to know what you are doing, that you are well! You are constantly in my thoughts, yet I sit down to write this letter to you with a heavy heart, for things do not go well for us here. Perhaps I shall even reach France before this letter? Or, it will reach France, but I shall not—'

The letter broke off there with an inky squiggle, as if he had been interrupted.

There was a woman, far to the north, beyond the mountains, a woman he loved. A sweetheart, a mistress, what did it matter?

'Nor should it matter, to me . . .' Mariana thought.

As she stared at the paper in her hand, the writing became blurred. She could no longer decipher the words. In their place, a female form, indistinct and faceless, hovered with a ghostly presence, as Mariana tried to imagine the distant Lisette.

Perhaps, for Guy also, Lisette's face was growing blurred and indistinct. He could not have seen her for three or four years. It was a long time for any girl to wait, especially for a soldier in time of war, with casualty lists growing longer daily.

Perhaps she hadn't waited, despite her letters.

Perhaps she had watched all the young men ride away, the resplendent cohorts of the gods of war, athirst for glory. Day by day, she had seen herself grow older, the bloom of youth fade. Perhaps she had looked in her mirror one morning and fancied a wrinkle or a grey hair, and decided to wait no more but accept the first suitable offer of a secure home with some middle-aged, undistinguished bridegroom. And on her wedding-night, in the darkness, she would pretend, her mind far away with another, surrendering her body but caring no longer.

Mariana sighed.

'It interests you, my correspondence?' a dry voice asked.

Mariana jumped up with a guilty start, the letter dropping from her hand and her cheeks burning.

Guy stood by the door. The shoulders of his green coat were dark with rain. It dripped from the mane of black horsehair adorning the brass dragoon helmet with its leopardskin binding which he held upside-down by the chinstrap of overlapping metal scales. He set the helmet down carefully on a table before pulling off his wet coat and hanging it over a chairback, grimacing as his actions pulled at the unhealed wound. In his shirt-sleeves and white waistcoat he came across to her and, reaching past her, picked up the letter. His wet hair clung to his scalp, and trickles of water ran down his temples and across the scar which gleamed lividly against his tanned skin.

'Beaudoin said you spoke good French,' he said,

in French this time. 'Why did you tell me differently?'

'I saw no reason to admit it,' Mariana replied defensively.

'You mean, you lied!' he said contemptuously.

He had been re-reading his own letter. Now, swiftly, he clapped his hands together, crushing the paper into a ball which he hurled across the room into a far corner, in a gesture which appeared to Mariana more eloquent than a host of words.

'I have been burying *my* dead!' he said abruptly.

'I know,' Mariana answered soberly. 'Beaudoin told me. I am so sorry about the lieutenant, truly.'

'More lies!' he said harshly. 'Why should you grieve? One French soldier less, isn't that what you want? Your only regret is that it is not *my* dead body lying out there in the wet earth. You would have preferred that, wouldn't you?'

'No . . .' Mariana whispered, white-faced before this uncharacteristic display of mingled grief and anger, and the searing bitterness of his voice.

A little timorously, but very earnestly, she added, 'Too many men have died already. Perhaps you don't believe me, but I pray you may live to return home, to France.'

'Home?' He gave a short, scornful laugh. 'We're an army in retreat, Mariana. They'll hang no flags out to welcome us! They'll bar their doors and windows and forget they stood in the streets and waved their hats and cheered when we rode off to war!' His tone changed. 'Etienne used to say there was not a bullet cast, or a sword forged, which would prevent him from getting back to France. He was right. It took the fever to do it. All the cards in the deck are marked, Mariana, and Fate always holds the winning hand.'

He sighed impatiently and began to pace up and down the room restlessly, as if he longed for action and found being denied it unbearable, fretting like a coursing hound which hears the huntsman's call and strains at the leash. When he began to speak again, it was jerkily, in bursts of nervous energy.

'I owe my life to Etienne, and to Beaudoin, did good Beaudoin tell you that? I don't suppose he did. But when I was wounded and unhorsed, left sprawling in the mud, it was Lieutenant Legrand and the sergeant who came galloping up, seized an arm apiece and dragged me off the field between them. If they hadn't, I should have been ridden down by the cavalry, either ours or theirs. So, you see,' he added awkwardly, as if he felt he had to justify his behaviour, 'I couldn't abandon Étienne either, although, in theory, I should have done. One can't allow oneself to be delayed for one sick man, or several. Those who cannot keep up, must be left behind—but not for them!'

The last words were spoken softly, almost to himself. He was standing by the window. 'Come over here!' he ordered suddenly.

Mariana crossed the room and waited uncertainly.

'Look up there,' he said, pointing. 'The rain is clearing, and you can just see the hilltops. Your Spanish patriots are up there, waiting, like carrion crows. They know we are few, and weak. They track us, as buzzards track an injured deer. *He* is there, somewhere, the White Wolf . . .'

Mariana started and looked up at his profile, sharply etched against the wet glass. The features were hard, as if cast in bronze, and his mouth had a vicious set to it which she had not seen before.

'How you hate him . . .' she whispered.

'I would do anything to take his victory from him!' he said in a quiet, fierce tone, 'I care nothing for the British, nothing for the rest of Spain. But if I could take that one man, alive . . .'

He seemed to recollect himself and broke off. 'Well?' he demanded roughly. 'What are you doing here, anyway? Or were you just prying?'

'I wasn't prying!' she denied. 'I was waiting for you. I want to know what you intend to do with me when you leave here.'

'You?' he replied rudely. 'You can stay here, or go home, or run away to your deserter in the hills—it's all one to me. Go and join your deserter. He's probably lonely by now, and hungry. You can take him his food, and afterwards you can let him make love to you on the heather.'

'Why did you have to say that?' Mariana demanded so vehemently that he turned to stare at her, his eyebrows raised in surprise. 'You're an educated man and an officer. Yet you choose to speak to me in a way which is deliberately insulting!'

'You think you're entitled to better treatment, I suppose?' he queried.

'Even from you,' she said quietly.

'You forget, señorita, I offered you a truce once, and you rejected it,' he said coolly. His grey eyes met hers with a directness which caused her to flush. That now familiar uncertainty began to creep over her.

'I haven't forgotten,' Mariana muttered, looking at the floor.

He took a few steps towards her. 'Look at me, Marianne,' he ordered. When she did not obey, he added quietly, 'I'm not a pretty sight, am I? My face distresses you.'

'No,' Mariana exclaimed, embarrassed. 'It doesn't trouble me at all!'

'Then you can look at me.' He tipped her chin up with his index finger and she looked up into his face with apprehension, dreading what he might say next.

'So, you think I behave badly towards you,' he went on. The grey eyes were steady and it seemed as if they could read not only her mind but her heart. 'How do you think any other man in my position would have treated someone like you, arrested at night in suspicious circumstances? I could have had you shot. Or I could have let those men have you. Instead, though you are obliged to stay here, it's hardly in circumstances of any great discomfort. Even a wardrobe of pretty dresses to amuse yourself with.'

Mariana's flush darkened even more. 'What do you want me to say to you?' she retorted. 'Thank you? You told me yourself, I owe you no thanks.'

'You owe me something!' he replied angrily.

'What?' Mariana demanded icily. 'The gift of my body as an act of gratitude? Is that what you want? I came here to ask you to let me go home, but you have my most solemn promise that I won't stoop to a sordid bargain for my liberty! Unless French officers are quite without any honour, you will let me go!'

He hesitated, evidently controlling his temper with some difficulty, then said shortly, 'I'm sorry. I can't do that. It is not a matter of honour, but one of prudence. I cannot guarantee your safety once you are no longer under my direct protection. For your own sake you will have to stay here till we leave, which will not be long. After that, it won't matter—either to you, or to me,' he concluded sarcastically.

'And in the meantime?' she demanded in a low voice.

'In the meantime,' he returned drily, 'I should warn you against overestimating the value of the coin in which you imagine I wish to be paid! I would be the first man to admit that both your beauty and your—other charms—are considerable.' He waved a general hand at her figure. 'However, they are not unique, and the coin we speak of may be had in any brothel, and surrendered with a good deal more enthusiasm and good will!'

'Then go to a brothel!' Mariana flung at him. 'I imagine you are accustomed to frequent such places!'

'I would,' he said bluntly, 'if there were any near

at hand. But this is the most remarkable village I was ever in—for virtue. Not a house of ill-repute in sight! However, I recall your father was *alcalde* here. He probably closed them all down and packed off all the girls to learn to be seamstresses!'

'And so I am to supply your wants?' Mariana enquired silkily.

'I don't see why you should refuse,' he retaliated sharply. 'And you needn't make it sound such a *corvée*. It's generally considered to be a pleasurable pastime. If everyone had your attitude, the human race would long have died out. Though I am not altogether certain of the truth of your attitude. Your virtue seems to be somewhat selective. I don't see why you should deny me what your deserter out there probably enjoys freely!'

'I have already told you,' Mariana managed to say with the greatest difficulty, 'that he is not my lover. But even if he were, that still would not give you the right to seduce me! You are nothing but a libertine!'

The tight control he had held on his anger snapped as she flung her accusation proudly at him. '*Seduce!*' he roared at her. 'A libertine?' He took a rapid step towards her. The half-healed scar on his face seemed to glow against the glistening skin, and his eyes blazed at her. 'You call *me* a libertine? What? Do you imagine I am some hero of the boudoir? Do you think I have fought in no skirmishes except between linen sheets? I am a killer of my fellow-men, Mariana! That is what I have been taught and trained to do, and I do it very well. It is my trade. I've served my apprenticeship, and now I am a master at it!'

Mariana, frightened by the passion of his tone and the emotion which burned in the grey eyes, opened her mouth but was unable to reply.

'But do you think that *I* am never tired of war?' he demanded of her. 'Do you think that I am different from any other man? That I lack normal reactions and desires? That I don't wish sometimes to forget everything that I have done—and will do yet—for the sake of the uniform I wear; to forget how many good men I have seen die, and boys like Étienne destined never to see their homes again, or even their twentieth birthdays?

'And do you not think, Mariana, that I would not prefer a few moments of relaxation with a beautiful woman? That I should not take what opportunities come my way? Don't pretend not to understand me, because I know you understand me very well! Those beautiful eyes of yours betray you, Mariana!

'I told you I'd wait,' he went on more quietly, though still breathing heavily. 'But time doesn't. With so little left, surely we can spend it more agreeably than by flinging insults at one another?' He shrugged his shoulders in that Gallic manner of his, and added calmly, 'I don't mind a few fireworks . . . some men like vapid, compliant women. I don't. You have spirit, which I like. An affair without it, is like a good dinner without the wine. A spirited woman offers a man a challenge. Everything she does acts on him like an apéritif,' he smiled slightly. 'It whets the appetite and arouses the senses. So, I'll ask you again, plainly—will you allow me to come to your room?'

Mariana took a step back, knowing that her uncertainty showed in her face. She shook her head. There were so many things she might have said, once, but now none of them seemed adequate, and she could only stare at him dumbly.

'What? No lecture on Spanish honour?' The grey eyes were gently ironical. 'You see? You don't have to be so aggressively virtuous all the time. Leave that to plain women, of which, alas, the world is very full. You've made your point. I understand it. I even respect it! You are like some rare and beautiful exotic orchid. If a man had such a thing in his possession, of course he would treat it with respect. He would appreciate its value. But he would expect to enjoy its beauty, too! I'm not a barbarian. Let me prove it to you.'

'You have not the slightest understanding of how I feel!' Mariana gasped, finding words at last in a rush of resentment at the casual amorality of his attitude. 'You speak of me as though I were an—an object of pleasure, and nothing more! There is nothing, nothing, which would persuade me willingly into your bed!'

The irony in the grey eyes became a little bitter. 'Perhaps I understand more than you do, Marianne. At least, I understand that life is short and that we must enjoy what we can, while we can. That's my philosophy, anyway.'

'It's not mine, Guy,' she told him evenly.

'Isn't it?' His voice hardened slightly. 'This

dress,' he said unexpectedly, indicating the gown she wore. 'It's very pretty, very modest, very suitable. Why didn't you wear it on the first morning when Beaudoin brought you to see me? Why did you wear that Spanish dress?'

'I—I wanted to wear something from my country,' Mariana faltered, 'because you were French . . .'

He shook his head. 'Wrong. You wanted to wear something attractive, because I was a man.' His fingers closed on the muslin fichu and slowly pulled it away from the low neckline of the gown.

'No, that's not so!' Mariana gasped, trying to retrieve the fichu; in vain, as he had tucked it away in his pocket. She was struck with horror at the implication of his misunderstanding. What she had intended as a patriotic gesture, he had seen as coquetry. But she should have expected such an interpretation from a Frenchman, she thought bitterly.

He smiled, dismissing her protest, and ran his finger across her lips lightly, preventing her from saying any more. It was a simple little gesture which set her senses tingling.

'Think of that splendid painted bedroom upstairs, going to waste,' he whispered. 'There's a bed for lovers, if ever I saw one. Better than heather, any day.'

He cupped his hands around her chin, turning her face up towards his, and lowered his head. She felt the warm pressure of his mouth on hers, and a strange weakness swept over her. Her heart began to pound wildly, and her body, sensing his need, responded with one of its own, as his hand slid caressingly across her bodice, closing on her breast.

The increasing urgency of his touch awoke her to her danger. At the same time, the memory of the letter she had found on his desk leapt into her mind. Were he capable of any affections, then they lay beyond the Pyrenees with the unseen Lisette. He had clearly stated how he viewed Mariana. He turned to her to fulfil the promptings of a physical need. He was a foreign soldier, and she was no more than a campaign diversion to be embraced in the casual love-making of the opportunist in a strange land.

Humiliated, she began to struggle furiously, and succeeded in tearing herself free of his grasp.

'I told you, never!' she cried. 'Never, never!' Tears, hot, angry and despairing, rose unbidden to her eyes, stinging the lids, and she turned her head so that he should not see her brush them away with her hand.

'You precious little prude!' he said in harsh contempt. 'I was wrong to think you a woman! You're nothing but a pretty wax doll!'

Mariana whirled to face him. 'I am a Spanish woman!' she shouted at him. 'And you are nothing but French scum!'

He swept up his hand as if to strike her and she stumbled back hurriedly before the dangerous light in his eyes.

But then he slowly let his hand fall back by his side. 'Then guard your Spanish virtue!' he said

insolently. 'Observe your tiresome Spanish eti-
quette! Play those tedious, drawn-out, amorous
games you Spaniards like so much with some poor
fellow moping under your balcony for months with
nothing but a smile to reward him! But you'll have
to find someone else to play them with you, because
I am not your man! I'm no Spanish *caballero*, and I
don't obey your rules of "look, admire, but don't
touch"! You'd do well to remember that, señorita,
and keep out of my way!'

He strode past her to the desk, flinging himself
down to sort the papers, ignoring her.

Mariana gathered up her skirts and ran to the
door, hating him, and hating herself more.

CHAPTER
SIX

IN THE Duchess's splendid bedroom it was chilly,
and Juana went downstairs to find out if there were
any form of heating to be had. This eventually
arrived in the shape of an iron brazier, a squat
tripod with a heavy lid pierced by holes. Filled with
smouldering wood, it sent out a certain amount of
heat and a great deal of greenish smoke, which
smelled appalling and sent Mariana coughing to the
furthest point in the room away from the fiery
monster.

'Open the window, Juana, for goodness sake.
We'll asphyxiate!' she cried irritably.

'If I open the window, Doña Mariana, the heat
will escape. Only wait a little while and the wood
will dry out and smoke less.'

'I shall be smoked like a side of bacon by then!'
Mariana waved her hand to dispel the smoke which
irritated her nose and lungs.

'Then go out in the corridor for a little, and when
you come back you'll find it much better,' Juana
insisted, poking more pieces of kindling into the
belly of the latter-day Baal, which rewarded her
efforts by crackling and spitting furiously within
itself, the sparks knocking imperiously on the iron

lid as if some demon of the fire called angrily to be let out.

'I'm going into the garden,' Mariana declared, seizing the thick woollen shawl she had worn on the night of her capture.

'Doña Mariana! Come back here! You'll take a chill!' shrilled Juana.

Ignoring her, Mariana flung the shawl over her head and escaped thankfully out into the garden. The air there was damp and the shreds of mist hung above the ground, but it was an improvement on the brazier's evil emanations.

She made her way across the wet grass towards the gravel path. It scrunched beneath her feet, sounding unnaturally loud in the surrounding silence as she went slowly towards the orange-grove. By the fountain she paused. Neptune and his sea-horses glistened wetly in the water which should have been their natural element, and of which they had so long been deprived. Mariana cast her mind back to the night of the ball, when she had first seen this house, as an impressionable fifteen-year-old. The fountains had been playing then, illuminated by hanging lanterns strung between the nearby bushes, like a fairyland. How desolate it looked now, and how desolate the grove of orange-trees, dark and uninviting, rain dripping from their boughs.

Mariana went on towards it nevertheless, and, as she reached it, stopped suddenly before a mound of freshly-turned earth beneath the first line of trees.

She had stumbled upon the last resting-place of

Étienne Legrand, for whom neither mother nor sweetheart need wait any longer in France. The grave was unmarked, probably to prevent its desecration by revengeful peasants, once the dragoons moved out. After their departure, no one would even know who slept here, so quietly and so peacefully, so far from the noise of battle, and from home.

Mariana turned aside with the vague intention of finding some foliage or even late autumnal flowers to place on the grave. But, as she did so, her ear caught a low whistle from within the trees, and she pulled the shawl about her and peered nervously into the gloom.

'Felipe?' she whispered.

There was a movement, and a man's shape materialised a few yards away from her. Even though she expected it to be he, his sudden appearance from among the dripping foliage made her start. It seemed so much his natural element, as though he had lost some human characteristic and become a creature of the wild.

'What happened yesterday?' he demanded without ceremony, coming up to her. 'What was all that shooting?'

'It was Paco. But I thought at first it was at you they fired,' she told him. 'I was so frightened, I almost betrayed us.'

Felipe took her hand and kissed it. 'You are all right?' he asked anxiously.

'Yes, yes!' she assured him.

'I was hidden over there,' he said, gesturing

briefly behind him, 'when they buried that one, this morning. I had a good look at your Captain Dupré. He stood no more than a few yards from me, and had no idea I was there!' Felipe chuckled, then pointed to the grave. 'Was *he* killed yesterday?'

'No, he had the fever, and died early this morning.'

'Fever? They have the fever?' Felipe demanded sharply.

'I know of only that one. Some of the others are wounded.'

Felipe pushed back his long black hair and surveyed her thoughtfully. There was something very direct and penetrating about his gaze which made Mariana grateful for the damp air which allowed her to pull her shawl about her face.

'Mariana,' he said slowly, 'yesterday I asked you to come with me, to the hills. I know we were interrupted, nevertheless, I could not help but notice a certain reluctance in your tone. I should like to think I was mistaken, but I begin to fear I was not.'

For all his courteous tone, a warning prickle ran over Mariana, an intimation of danger.

'I don't want to be a nuisance to you, Felipe,' she said as evenly as possible. 'And I should be, in the hills.'

'You know my feelings for you?' he asked, in the same quiet tone.

'Yes, Felipe, I know,' Mariana acknowledged awkwardly.

'But I am not sure of your feelings for me,' he said. 'Forgive me if I am unjust, but occasionally, recently, I have begun to wonder whether you do love me.'

'I have never been untrue to you, Felipe!' Mariana exclaimed. 'I swear it!'

She knew he wanted her to say, 'I love you', but she could not. She forced herself to look up into his eyes and was struck by how much they resembled those of a wild beast, alert, watchful, suspicious and enigmatic.

'I swear it, Felipe,' she repeated firmly. 'Don't accuse me of disloyalty.'

'Then if you love me,' he said slowly, watching her face closely, 'will you do something for me, and for your country?'

'You know I've always done everything I could to help,' Mariana reminded him. 'What is it you want now?'

As she asked this, she strove to keep the tremor of indecision from her voice, knowing that what he was about to ask of her was not only an act of patriotism: it was an act that would serve as a touchstone for her love for him. If she failed the test, he would know the truth at last.

'*I want that man, Dupré* . . .' Felipe said softly.

Mariana stared at him, hardly understanding. 'You want Captain Dupré? What do you mean?' she stammered at last.

Felipe reached out and grasped her shoulders, leaning towards her intently. 'Mariana—that man has information about the latest French move-

ments, about the numbers of troops being with-
drawn. That information must be obtained for the
British! We *need* him—and *you* can bring him to
us!'

'I?' she cried out loudly, stepping back and
wrenching herself free of his grip.

'Don't be alarmed!' he urged. 'I have thought it
all out carefully. You will be in no danger. All you
have to do is tell the Frenchman the story I shall
give you. Nothing more! Your part will consist
solely in finding a suitable moment to whisper it
into his ear.' He smiled slightly. 'You are beautiful,
Mariana, and clever. You'll find a way to do it. The
rest can be left to me.'

'But, Felipe!' she protested. 'He isn't going to
believe some fantastic tale from me, of all people!'

'Yes, he will,' Felipe said calmly. 'I watched him
this morning, Mariana, when they threw the earth
into that open grave. He wept. But with the last
shovel of soil his face changed. He put his grief
behind him. Now he wants action, he wants to
prove he is not beaten! He's impatient, and angry,
Mariana, and that makes him vulnerable!'

'Even if that's so,' Mariana said shakily. 'He's
not a fool.'

Felipe shrugged. 'No—but the cleverest man can
be the victim of his own vanity. I doubt our captain
is made of wood. The French soldier fights like a
devil, but he goes down like a painted skittle before
a pair of melting eyes.'

'You want me to encourage his advances!'
Mariana cried incredulously. 'I won't do it!'

'No!' Felipe snarled. 'Do you think *I* would ask that of you? I swear to you, if he so much as touches a hair of your head, I'll kill him with these two hands!'

He lifted up his hands before her, lean and blackened like a gipsy's from his four years in the wild.

'But that will not be necessary, Mariana, not if you are clever. Will you do it? Will you do it for Spain, for Miguel—and for me?'

'I, too, am a Spanish patriot, Felipe,' she said quietly. 'But I don't like this. You're asking me to betray this man, aren't you?'

'Betrayal?' Felipe cried angrily. 'It is Spain which was betrayed! Have you forgotten that? Have you forgotten Miguel, your own brother, and how he died? You are a Spanish woman, and Dupré is your enemy!'

'No, I haven't forgotten!' she flung at him. She twisted her hands nervously together, debating the matter feverishly in her mind. 'What would you do with him if you were to capture him?'

'That hardly concerns you, Mariana,' Felipe said, his voice gently reproachful. 'Your part is simply to plant an idea in his head.'

'But I want to know. I have a right to be told,' she maintained obstinately.

She had never argued with Felipe before. She had never had the courage. But now she stared at him directly, and, as if disconcerted by the frank gaze of her hazel eyes, Felipe spread out his hands appeasingly.

'What would you have me do with him?' he enquired courteously.

'Treat him as a prisoner of war, and hand him over to the British!' Mariana's expression was determined. 'And I want your word on it.'

'But of course!' he exclaimed. 'What did you imagine?'

Mariana sighed in relief. 'I'm sorry, Felipe. I know you to be a man of honour. It's just . . . I've never done anything like this before. I want to understand exactly what I shall be doing.'

Felipe took her hand and squeezed her fingers reassuringly. 'Don't you trust me?'

'Yes—yes, of course I do, Felipe!' Mariana said earnestly.

He smiled, and she wished she could find it reassuring, but there was something wolf-like in that smile.

'What is it I am to tell him?' she asked hesitantly.

'He would like to capture the White Wolf, you say?' Felipe laughed to himself. 'Though he never had a better opportunity than he did this morning, had he but known it! Well, I'm a generous man, I'll give him a second chance to lay his hands on me. You see, Mariana, you will bait the trap with a lure he cannot resist—you will offer to lead him to the White Wolf!'

Bending down towards her so that his long black hair brushed her face, Felipe outlined the details of the story she was to tell, making her repeat it until he was satisfied.

'Remember,' he said when it was done. 'I rely on

you and Spain relies on you, Mariana.' He touched her cheek lightly with his fingers. 'Don't fail me, my dear . . .'

Mariana walked slowly in from the garden. So that was it, the test of her loyalty, and of her love. The house loomed up in front of her, grey in the twilight. She remembered her father, when she had been very small, opening the cupboard which had housed his collection of antiquities, and showing her a fragment of Roman mosaic.

'Do you see how many tiny pieces make up the whole, Mariana?' he had asked. 'Some are important key pieces, and some are only plain background. But each of them is indispensable, and without any one of them the whole piece is incomplete. A man's life, and his actions, are the same. He may be only the most insignificant part of the whole, but his every action matters. Judge what you do carefully, Mariana, or others will judge it for you!'

How much she would have valued her father's guidance now, she thought sadly as she entered the great house.

In the entrance hall, she pulled the shawl from her head and shook it out. Spots of moisture flew through the air. Mariana looked about her, hearing voices. The doors to the gilded ballroom were half open, and through them she could see a group of men, sitting or crouching on the floor in a circle. Their stained uniforms and unshaven faces made them an incongruous sight amidst the gold and white splendour. One of the huge mirrors on the ballroom wall reflected the group so that she could see their faces, dirty, lively, intent—all watching Michel Boucher who, on his knees, leaned forward, shaking his clenched fist, and threw something on the scuffed parquet floor in the middle of the group.

The rattle of the dice echoed on the wood. There was a roar from the onlookers and a burst of laughter. One or two voices called out witticisms, followed by more laughter.

Some of those men had formed the burial party which, early that day, had dug the lonely grave in the orange-grove. Yet others had grimy bandages wound about head or leg or arm. But now they were off duty, and gambling away pay they had probably not yet even received. The French lines of communication hardly existed any more. Yet to listen to the men now, laughing and joking, one would have thought they hadn't a care in the world.

Mariana crept past the doorway. Intent on their pastime, none of them noticed her. She did not want to go upstairs, where the simpering painted Psyche and the enraptured pink face of the Cupid mocked her from the ceiling above. Instead, she made her way to the little chapel.

It was deserted and quiet. There was a faint smell of old incense and of wax. Before a painting of St Barbara, a dish held the remains of the candle lit by Juana in a pious bid to avert the thunderstorm, a blackened wick in a blob of cold wax.

By the wall, near to the altar, was a prayer-stool, upholstered in red velvet, of the kind the French call a *prie-dieu*. It could be a chair or, reversed and the hinged seat turned up, a place to kneel and pray. Here the Duchess made her devotions when she was in residence. Mariana turned it into a chair and sat down.

She was twenty years of age, and had never believed herself to be in love. She had begun to feel she was unnatural. Nearly all the childhood friends of her age were now married women. Some had families of two or three little children. Girls flower into early maturity beneath the Southern sun. They married at fourteen, fifteen. But for the intervention of the war, she herself would have been married these five years to Felipe, and borne his children. He had first promised to marry her on the night of the ball, out there in the garden beneath the hanging lanterns; seeing him then, with the eyes of a fifteen-year-old, how flattered she had been. And now? Mariana tried to imagine herself as a bride, standing before an altar like the one before which she sat, standing there with Felipe.

Felipe. A tremor of repugnance ran over her. Yet, if all went well, that was how it would all end. She would be the bride of the White Wolf—no longer a hunted man, but a victor who had come down from the hills to claim his reward for his four years of living like an animal among men little better than brutes. She was that reward—he demanded no other prize but her hand in marriage. But that he claimed as a right. She belonged to him.

He had earned her. She was his.

'They brand felons,' Mariana thought. 'They might as well brand me. I carry the mark of Felipe Marquez. No other man in the whole of Spain would dare to raise his eyes to me.'

But there was one man, not a Spaniard . . . Mariana sighed and leant her head against the cool plaster wall.

From the back of the chapel came a faint creak of a hinge and the sound of a footstep. Mariana froze. Someone had entered. She turned her head slowly, keeping the rest of her body taut.

Michel Boucher, believing himself alone, came slowly down the chequered aisle, his boots scraping on the decorative tiles. He looked sullen. No doubt the dice had fallen badly for him, and his button eyes were fixed greedily on the altar on which stood a pair of silver gilt candlesticks.

He climbed the chancel steps and stretched out his hand to the nearer candlestick. Carefully he examined it, turning it this way and that. With a grunt of satisfaction, he stowed it away in his pocket and reached for its pair.

'Put those back!' Mariana ordered him.

Startled, Boucher let the second candlestick drop and spun round with an oath. When he saw who it was, his face took on an expression first of relief, and then of enmity.

'You keep your mouth shut and mind your own affairs!' he said sourly. He turned his back to her and retrieved the fallen candlestick.

Mariana jumped up and ran to the altar, grasping

his sleeve to prevent him from putting this find also in his pocket.

'How dare you touch church plate? If you have no religion, then at least show some respect!'

He shook her away roughly. 'That's right, I've no religion. At the revolution, they chased the priests out of France, and to my mind they did right. Now the Emperor has let them all back again. That's his business. My ideas haven't changed! And if you don't want to get hurt, stay over there and keep quiet!'

'I am not afraid of you.' As she spoke, Mariana realised that it was true. She didn't fear him at all. Perhaps she should, but a calm certainty filled her. The confidence of her voice shook him, and he began to look less sure of himself.

'I believe,' she said scornfully, 'that you are no better than a common thief! Before you were a dragoon, it wouldn't surprise me if you'd seen the inside of more than one gaol.'

'Well now, aren't you a clever young lady?' he returned sarcastically, but he looked badly shaken.

'My father was *alcalde* here, and administered the law,' she informed him coldly. 'He dealt with rogues and felons. I know what they look like. From here they went in chains to the galleys.'

Boucher paled slightly and rubbed his mouth with the back of his hand. His little black eyes flickered furtively, as if seeking escape.

'Put the candlesticks back!' Mariana ordered him. 'Go on!'

'And if I don't?' he demanded hoarsely.

'I shall make it my business to see you are charged with the theft of church plate and punished. I shall insist upon it to Captain Dupré.'

She saw the uncertainty and fear in Boucher's eyes. He was not sure that she could carry out her threat. But neither was he sure that she couldn't. Slowly he drew the candlesticks from his pockets and set them back on the altar.

'There, then,' he said sullenly. 'See how long they stay there! If I don't have them, another will.'

He turned and made off down the aisle towards the door of the chapel. When he reached it, he paused and called out viciously:

'You wait! You'll regret it. And don't think you'll always have the captain to protect you! Every man here is waiting for the day he tires of you!'

Mariana affected to ignore him, and set the candlesticks in their rightful place, surveying them thoughtfully.

He was right, of course. If he didn't take them, another would. When the French left, so would these candlesticks. But she could prevent that if she herself hid them. But where? The chapel offered no place which would not be searched. She would smuggle them upstairs to her room, and seek a hiding-place there. She felt a responsibility to see that these candlesticks, at least, did not cross the Pyrenees in a soldier's knapsack.

Mariana lifted them down, having first glanced cautiously about her to make sure she was not observed, and rolled them carefully in her shawl.

Holding the bundle tightly, she felt herself out of the chapel and made her way quickly to her room.

It was not difficult to do so unobserved, for the daylight was fading now and the staircase was in gloom. She would have to call Juana to light the candles.

But when she pushed open the door of the painted bedroom, she found this was unnecessary. A golden glow bathed the room from a branched candalabrum on a small table. High above, Cupid and Psyche floated in a velvet dusk. The shutters were closed and the stove had gone out, blessedly, but its warmth lingered.

Guy was lying stretched out on the bed, propped up comfortably against the satin pillows which he had piled conveniently behind his head. His coat hung on the cheval glass, and his shirt was unbuttoned, revealing the tanned skin of his chest. One long leg trailed over the side of the bed and the other was crooked up in front of him, his boot scraping the smooth coverlet into a ridge.

'Come in,' he invited her. 'Don't stand in the doorway.'

'What are you doing? Get out of here!' Mariana exclaimed.

'Waiting for you,' Guy told her with an impudent grin.

His voice sounded different, far removed from the tone of caustic insolence that he had employed at the close of their earlier conversation. He himself seemed somehow different, too, quite relaxed and at his ease, untroubled by her obvious agitation.

'What's that you've got there?' he asked, pointing at the shawl in Mariana's arms.

She flushed. 'It's nothing.'

'Then put the wretched thing down. You look as though you're nursing a baby.' He chuckled.

Mariana's embarrassment increased and she set the bundle down hastily on the nearest chair. To add to her confusion, it unwrapped itself and the candlesticks fell to the floor with an unearthly clatter.

'I'm surprised you managed to find those,' he said, raising his eyebrows. 'That kind of thing usually disappears first.'

'I'm not stealing them!' Mariana denied hotly. 'I'm hiding them, to prevent them disappearing.'

'I've been hunting about, too,' he said, unperturbed. 'I went down into the cellars. See what I found!'

He reached down to the floor beside him and held up a cobwebby bottle.

'Good wine—from the noble lady's private store.'

Mariana's heart sank in dismay.

He was drunk.

It explained the difference in his manner and the faint slurring of his voice. Worse, it offered an ominous explanation for his presence here.

To hide her consternation, she stooped to retrieve the candlesticks and made a great play of placing them on the dressing-table.

'And,' he continued, reaching to the floor again, 'I brought two glasses. One for you—and one for me.'

'I don't want any, Guy.' Mariana watched him wrench the cork from the bottle with increasing apprehension. 'You shouldn't be here . . .'

'It's an insult to refuse to drink with a man,' Guy said obstinately. He sat up and swung his other leg to the floor and with studied concentration filled the two glasses.

'Only for another man to refuse to drink with him, not for a woman.'

'I've yet to see you behave as a woman,' he muttered.

'Will you go?' Mariana cried.

'No. Come over here and join me.' He patted the space on the bed beside him.

'Where is Juana?' she asked nervously, drawing further back.

'I gave a couple of bottles to Beaudoin. Now he and your maid have resolved their differences and are growing nicely merry in the kitchen, where she is sitting on his knee.' He gave her his twisted grin. 'That, *querida*, is called a diversionary attack.'

'How much of that have you drunk already?' Mariana asked desperately, seeing her fate sealed more surely with every word he spoke.

'Enough to kill the pain in my ribs.' He got to his feet and strolled lazily across the room to stand in front of her. 'We shall move out in the morning,' he said. 'You can share a farewell glass of wine with me, can't you? We might even share a little . . . companionship.'

'Please, Guy, I want you to leave!' Mariana pleaded breathlessly.

He put his hands gently on her shoulders, shaking his head. 'Not this time, *querida*, this time I'm staying.'

'No, Guy, you're not!' she insisted. 'You should go. You shouldn't drink any more—and I'm not going to drink with you!'

He ignored her protests and began to take the tortoiseshell comb and pins from her hair. The topknot fell down in curling chestnut locks, framing her pale face.

'Don't look so frightened,' he whispered. 'I won't hurt you . . . I'm not a novice or some clumsy peasant.'

He ran his hands down the silken length of her hair and slipped his arms around her rigid body, drawing her towards him.

She knew she should resist, must resist. But the world seemed a topsy-turvy sort of place in which the warmth of the room, the golden haze of the candlelight and scent of melting wax, combined with the nearness of him, the touch of his hand, the caress of his breath against her cheek, succeeded in paralysing her will as effectively as they sent her senses reeling.

She felt her stiff body become pliable in his embrace, moulding itself against his, and as his mouth found hers, every objection seemed to melt away and she knew only that she wanted him desperately, wanted him to hold her tightly, never to release her. That she wanted to belong to him, to be a part of him, and of no other.

No other. Like a sudden drenching with cold water, the memory of Felipe flooded over her.

'No, Guy, no!' she begged in agonised tones, twisting her head aside so that he could not kiss her. 'You must go, please! Leave my room . . .'

He bent his head and gently kissed the throbbing pulse in her white throat. 'Trust me, Marianne . . .' he murmured into her ear. There was a slight tremor in his voice and she could smell the wine on his breath. 'You won't be sorry. It will be all right, you'll see . . .'

Trust me. Felipe had said that. As for this man, there could be no trust, there could be nothing, between them—ever.

His exploring fingers had found the hooks at the back of the gown and fumbled at them.

'Why won't you listen to me?' she pleaded wildly. 'I don't want you to make love to me!'

He looked up. The grey eyes were warm, their colour softened to a greyish blue.

'Yes, you do,' he said. His voice was quite sober now, his speech steady and clear. 'Yes, you do, Marianne. I am not a fool. I should not be here if I didn't understand that.'

He knew. He had sensed her body grow soft in his arms, divined that need in her which she herself refused to admit. The knowledge, that he understood, burned in her like a searing flame of degradation and dishonour.

'I don't!' Mariana cried out. 'And I won't!'

She began to struggle in his embrace, but he tightened his grip, refusing to release her, and she knew it was useless. With a sudden movement he swept her up into his arms and carried her over to the Duchess's splendid bed, and set her down gently on the satin pillows.

'Guy, no . . .' she moaned, putting up her hands to ward him away as he sank down beside her, his arm flung across her stomach.

'You refused me before, and I accepted it,' he said huskily. He was breathing heavily and his eyes shone with that almost feverish light. 'But not this time . . .'

Mariana tried to roll away from beneath him as he bent towards her, but he grasped at her shoulder and the rose silk of the gown tore beneath his fingers. Panting, she pushed at his face, almost sobbing in her panic. For a moment she was tempted to strike at his injured ribs, but even as the thought entered her mind, she knew it would be a terrible mistake.

'Why won't you believe me?' she cried out in despair.

'Because I know it isn't true! You do want me!' he declared fiercely. His long strong fingers grasped her chin, forcing her to look up at his face, which glistened with tiny beads of perspiration. 'Tell me, Marianne, tell me you don't want me, and make me believe it!'

'I don't want you,' Mariana whispered. She summoned all the strength she could pour into her faltering voice and repeated, with growing firmness, 'I don't want you!'

Anger and pain and despair surged up in her, culminating in a desire to hurt him, to strike at him with words, if not with her fists, to make him comprehend how great a barrier separated them.

'My family has lived for two hundred years in this place! Its men have always been brave and chivalrous—and its women virtuous! Yes, virtuous! That quality you despise so much! As for chivalry, that is something beyond your comprehension! You would treat me like a common whore! A piece of stolen booty like those candlesticks. There to be taken! But I am not here for you to take!'

'It's because of him,' he snarled at her. 'Answer me, damn you! It is, isn't it? That miserable deserter, skulking out there on that god-forsaken hillside!'

'It is not because of him!' Mariana struggled to a sitting position.

'You lie!' he said bitterly. His face changed, becoming harsh and unyielding. 'You've lied to me from the start, you little trollop! Well, you're wrong if you imagine I'm going to slink out of here like a whipped dog. He can have you back—if he still wants you—but not until I've finished with you!'

He thrust her roughly back on to the pillows, throwing himself across her and, holding her down with one hand, grasped at her skirt with the other.

Terrified at the vengeful look in his eyes,

Mariana snatched at her only chance to divert him from his purpose.

'Listen to me, Guy, Listen! If you'll go and leave me alone, and not—not touch me, I'll help you—'

'Help me?' He stared at her. Then, suddenly, he threw back his head and began to laugh.

'You would like, wouldn't you, to capture the White Wolf?' Mariana said deliberately.

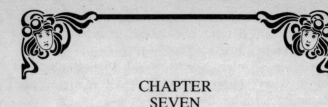

CHAPTER
SEVEN

GUY STOPPED laughing.

'What did you say?' He gripped her arms so tightly that she cried out in pain, and shook her as a terrier shakes a rat. 'What did you say?' he shouted.

'Let go, Guy, you're hurting me!' she gasped.

He drew a shuddering breath and released her. 'Go on,' he ordered her in a low, tightly controlled voice. 'What do you know of the White Wolf?'

Mariana rubbed her arms where he had gripped her and whispered hastily, 'I don't know where he is! But I know of someone who would know. I can take you to him.'

There was a silence, and Guy ran the tip of his tongue over his lips. 'Who is he?' he demanded hoarsely.

'His name is José Herrera. He's the local ne'er-do-well, a smuggler before the war, and perhaps still. When my father was *alcalde* here, he often had to deal with José, that's how I know him. Besides, he's a relative of my maid, Juana.'

She saw the Frenchman was listening closely, and continued in haste, the words spilling out in the story Felipe had told her to tell.

'If the White Wolf is hereabouts, anywhere, José will know. I'll send a message to him through Juana. I'll ask José to meet you.'

'He's a Spaniard. Why should he give me this information, supposing that he has it?' Guy asked shrewdly.

He was very pale, his cheeks appearing more sunken, and the look in his eyes was that of the hunter who sees his quarry suddenly break cover.

'Because he owes much to my family. My father was always lenient with him. He rather liked José. He used to say José was a rogue but not a villain. If *I* ask José to tell you what he knows, I'm sure he will do it.'

Guy hesitated, rubbing at his chin nervously with his thumb-nail. But she knew she had won. It was the bait, as Felipe had cunningly predicted, which the Frenchman could not refuse, which at this moment superseded even the desire to possess her.

'Very well,' Guy said abruptly. He stood up from the bed and went to take his coat from where it hung on the cheval glass. 'I'll delay our departure for twenty-four hours to enable you to arrange a meeting for me with this José Herrera.' He paused. 'Don't lie to me, *querida*,' he said quietly. 'God help you if you lie to me!'

Mariana shivered. 'I'm not lying! I'll do it. Juana shall go down to the village tonight and leave a message for José.'

The captain nodded. 'All right. I agree.' He strode to the door and pulled it open. 'Oh,' he glanced over his shoulder towards her. 'I leave you the wine!'

He went out, and the door closed on him.

Mariana sank back on the crushed satin pillows, pushing down her crumpled skirts, and drew a deep breath. Fate had played strangely into her hands. The trap was set. Now to persuade the prey to enter it.

'If you do not go alone, José will not meet you!' Mariana insisted.

'Señorita, I have not the slightest intention of riding out alone, in French uniform, with only a pretty girl to protect me!' Guy returned grimly. 'That trooper comes with us. I like to know who's watching my back!'

He indicated Boucher, who grinned malevolently at Mariana and gave a meaningful pat to the carbine strapped to his saddle.

'I have gone to great trouble to arrange this meeting for you,' Mariana argued. 'It was far from easy. You risk ruining it all. José insisted that only I come with you.'

'When we reach the rendezvous, the trooper will stay back out of sight,' Guy conceded. 'But he's coming along!'

With this compromise they had set out. It was early evening. The thunderstorms of earlier in the week had served to clear the air and the day had been a beautiful one, a last reminder of summer, with the sun shining down from a cloudless heaven.

The wrong weather altogether for treachery, Mariana reflected miserably as she rode beside Guy. Treachery should be played out against a backdrop of a lowering black sky. The three of them rode out now, as to a picnic, yet her heart had never been so heavy. The mountains were startlingly clear in the evening air. By a trick of the light, the vista was foreshortened, and they appeared only a step away.

The mule plodded sulkily along as though it disliked the superior company of the two cavalry horses. Mariana glanced over her shoulder. Boucher rode some three lengths behind them. Seeing her look back at him, an expression of sardonic mockery crossed his face.

'If anything goes wrong,' thought Mariana, 'I am the one Boucher will shoot. He would dearly like the excuse to kill me.'

Beside her, Guy spoke unexpectedly, in a strained voice, his eyes fixed on the road ahead.

'Last night,' he began, 'I was drunk—'

'I want nothing from you, Captain Dupré,' Mariana interrupted stonily, 'and that includes your apologies. We made an agreement. You kept your part, by refraining from molesting me further. I am keeping my part of our bargain by taking you to meet José Herrera. I don't want to refer to last night again.'

Guy did not attempt to reply to this. After a while, he rubbed the perspiration from his face with the back of his hand and said, 'Tell me more about this Herrera.'

'There is little I can tell you about José that I've not told you already. He's a smuggler. In the mountains, that's considered quite a respectable occupation. The people who practise it would be mortally offended to be called criminals. They consider it a perfectly legitimate profession to which the authorities unreasonably object! That's why my father was always lenient with José. He used to say, "José is a rogue, but you could give him a purse of gold to hold for you, and he would return it without the smallest coin missing."'

Guy grunted. 'How much further?'

'Not far. Just around the bend ahead. You'll be able to see the farm. It's only a very small, poor, place.'

Guy looked around him at the gently rising slopes of the Pyrenean foothills, purple with heather and dotted with tall bright green pine-trees, stiff and straight like sentries on the hillsides.

'It's deserted countryside,' he muttered, not to her, but to himself.

'That's why José chose it. He does not altogether trust the French. That is why I'm here, with you.'

It was proving all too easy to talk to him in this way, to assume a confidence she did not feel, and counter his misgivings. 'I have a talent for betrayal,' she mused. Then she thought, angrily, 'It is not betrayal! It is for Spain! Felipe will not harm him, he gave me his word. He will take him to the British. The British treat their prisoners well.'

'And he has the information I want?' Guy demanded abruptly.

'He spends all his life in the hills. A rabbit could not cross them without José knowing. If the man you seek is anywhere near here, José will have seen signs of his presence.'

Their conversation was interrupted, much to Mariana's relief, by the appearance, round the bend ahead, of the diminutive form of a very small donkey bearing an even smaller boy, trotting rapidly towards them.

'Hey there, *petit*!' Guy hailed him as he drew level. 'Is there anyone up ahead?'

The child stared at him solemn faced, with large brown eyes, and shook his head. He wore a ragged shirt and breeches, and his bare feet hung down on either side of his small mount's barrel body. A battered straw hat crowned his unkempt hair and he was armed with a stout stick.

'Where have you come from?' Guy persisted. 'Here . . .' He fished in his pocket and took out a small coin which he held out to the boy.

A gleam appeared in the urchin's eye, but he did not take the coin.

Guy repeated his question, and this time the boy said, 'Santa Maria de los Pirineos.'

'That's a mouthful,' Guy observed. He turned to Mariana. 'Do you know it?'

She nodded. 'It's a tiny village, way off the road, high up in the hills.'

'You ask him where he's going,' Guy instructed her. 'My uniform puts him off.'

Mariana asked him.

'To my grandfather's,' the urchin said. He

pointed in the direction from which they had come.
'Down there.'

'Ask him, has he seen anyone on the way,' Guy
said quietly.

'No one, señorita,' the child said when she trans-
lated this question.

'Go on, then,' Guy told him, and made to toss
the coin to him.

But the urchin immediately belaboured the
donkey's flanks with his stick and set off down the
road at a fine pace.

'He didn't want the money!' Guy exclaimed in
surprise.

'They are mountain people. They are proud,'
Mariana explained. She could have added, 'They
want no charity from the French,' but she did not.

They rounded the bend ahead and reined in. The
road, a stony track, fell away from them, downhill.
At the bottom of the slope, in a sort of hollow,
stood a small whitewashed house of the kind to be
seen in any Spanish village, except that here it
stood alone. It had a roof of rust-coloured tiles and
a balcony on the upper floor laden with geraniums
in pots. A vine grew up over the doorway, and a
rough, home-built table and stools standing before
the door indicated that the occupants were in the
habit of sitting outside their dwelling of an evening.
A dilapidated outhouse or two and a pen holding
three goats completed the picture. Apart from the
goats, the only sign of life was a colony of chickens,
scratching in the dust of the courtyard. Of human
life there was no sign at all.

'Too quiet,' muttered Boucher uneasily.

Guy glanced up at the surrounding hillsides still bathed in the evening sun, but where the shadows cast by the tall pine-trees were lengthening rapidly.

'We'll wait here for a little,' he said, 'and watch.'

The horses and the mule stood patiently, shaking their heads occasionally to dislodge the troublesome flies, and swishing their tails. After ten minutes the door of the house opened, and the two dragoons stiffened. But it was an old woman who came out, crook-backed and black-clad. She was carrying a dish and began to scatter food to the chickens which ran fussily to greet her. They watched her finish her task and shuffle to one of the rickety sheds about the yard and go inside. She came out with a pail, and going to the pen which held the goats, settled down to milk them.

'If you like, I'll go down first,' Mariana offered. The waiting and watching were unbearable. Her stomach churned and she felt ill with nervous tension.

'I'll come with you,' Guy said, apparently reaching a decision. He turned in the saddle to Boucher. 'Stay here and don't take your eyes off that farmyard or the hills behind it. Watch especially for birds flying up suddenly. If you see anything at all move out there, fire a single shot.'

'Don't worry, Captain,' Boucher nestled his carbine in the crook of his arm. 'I'll keep my eyes skinned.'

'You'd better! It's your neck too!' Guy growled.

He shook the reins and set off at a brisk trot down

the stony track to the farm, Mariana following.

The old woman must have seen them approach, but she ignored them, continuing her milking as if the girl and the dragoon were of no consequence. They reined up before the door of the house, and Mariana called out, 'José! Are you there? It's Señorita Alvarez de las Fuentes.'

The door creaked open and the low rectangle was filled by the massive form of José, with his black eye-patch and shaggy head. Guy gave an exclamation, and Mariana said hastily, 'Don't be alarmed by the look of him!'

'You might have warned me that we were going to meet a creature, half man and half bear!' he muttered.

'Welcome, Doña Mariana!' José said affably. 'Bring the Frenchman inside.'

Guy dismounted and held up his arms to Mariana to lift her down from the mule. She looked down at him and hesitated. She seemed to see them both in a kind of frozen picture, as if for a moment time were suspended.

The brass dragoon helmet, gleaming in the evening sun, cast a shadow over his eyes and the bridge of his nose, and only his firm chin and sensitive mouth were illuminated by the golden light. Even the scar on the right-hand side of his face was mostly obscured by the chinstrap of overlapping metal scales. He was an enemy soldier, and he looked it. Yet those arms, now reaching up to help her, had held her close. Those hands had caressed her body and that mouth had kissed her, and the memory of its warm demanding pressure had become a part of her.

It was a memory she must resolutely crush. She had a duty to perform, a duty to her country. But she had a feeling of impending disaster, a crawling sensation up and down her spine as if unseen eyes were fixed on them. It was still not too late. A word, one word, of warning . . .

'It is Boucher,' she thought. 'I sense him up there, watching us.'

She put her hands resolutely on Guy's broad shoulders and allowed him to swing her to the ground. He managed this easily enough, but with a faint hiss of breath between his teeth, and she remembered the unhealed injury which plagued him.

They followed José into the house. Inside it was dim, cool and primitively furnished. The floor was of beaten earth, and from the ceiling and around the whitewashed walls hung all manner of commodities, from strings of onions and garlic heads, and ropes of dried sausages and bacon, to domestic and farmyard implements and harness. It was like entering a grove of weird and wonderful stalactites.

'¡*Aquí tiene Usted su casa*' José said politely. 'This house is yours!' He gestured politely to a chair and Mariana sat down.

'I have no time to waste!' Guy said curtly. 'The lady tells me you spend much time in the hills.'

'I am a poor man,' José said blandly, 'and must earn my living.' He unhooked a goatskin gourd from the wall and held it up. 'Wine, Captain?'

'I appreciate your hospitality,' Guy returned tersely, 'but I'd appreciate your information more.'

From outside there came a faint clatter.

'It is the old woman, tending the goats. She is my aunt,' said José smoothly. He held up the gourd and, tilting it, threw back his head, opened his mouth and poured the rough wine straight down in a red stream. Then he wiped his mouth with his hand, spat on the floor and asked, 'What is it you want to know, Frenchman? And remember! Whatever I tell you, I tell you for the sake of this lady and her saintly parents, God rest their souls.' José crossed himself devoutly.

'I understand,' Guy said. 'I want—'

He broke off as the crack of a single shot echoed on the air, followed by the wild drumming of hoofs nearing the house.

'Boucher!' Guy exclaimed.

He leapt to his feet, but before he could reach the door it was flung open and the evening sunlight blotted out by a newcomer.

They all stood as if struck powerless, staring at the man in the doorway who, ducking his head of long, tangled back hair beneath the lintel, came into the room, letting the door close behind him.

'Felipe!' Mariana cried, running forward and putting her hand on his arm, though whether to greet him, or to prevent his entering further, she could not have said.

He smiled slightly and, raising her hand to his lips, kissed her fingertips.

'My heart is yours,' he said softly to her, 'and the sight of you my reward. If I have ever doubted your love for me, forgive me. I shall never doubt it again.'

Mariana stared at him, white-faced and unable to speak. She heard Guy, behind her, draw in his breath sharply.

'And this, I suppose,' he said in an oddly constricted voice, 'is your deserter in the hills!'

'This, Frenchman,' José said, baring his blackened teeth in a grin, 'is the White Wolf!'

Felipe bowed politely. 'I am honoured, Captain, that you will be our guest. I heard you had a desire to meet me. You see the efforts I have made to oblige you.'

Mariana knew that Guy's eyes were on her, and she forced herself to turn slowly and meet his gaze, unable to keep her shame from showing in her own. Ignoring the two *guerrilleros*, Guy took a step towards her.

'Tell me,' he said, and his voice was still constricted, as if he had difficulty in forming the words he wanted. 'Tell me you did not plan this, Marianne. Say you did not, and I shall believe you.'

The grey eyes were fixed on her, waiting, waiting for her denial. When she said nothing, he burst out, 'For God's sake, tell me, did you know?'

'I knew . . .' she whispered wretchedly.

The muscles of his face twitched, and he gave a long drawn-out sigh.

'I should have realised that you would be his

woman!' he said bitterly. 'That first night, I should
have had Beaudoin put a bullet in your scheming,
treacherous, lying little brain!'

José strode forward and struck the captain a
vicious blow which sent him staggering back against
the crude wooden table, blood streaming from his
split lip.

'Mind your tongue, Frenchman, or I will cut it
out!' he growled. 'The lady is a patriot—a loyal
daughter of Spain!'

The gourd had fallen to the floor and, as it fell,
the wine splashed out, marking the hem of
Mariana's skirt with red spots. The remainder
seeped out into the earthen floor in a widening dark
stain.

'Blood . . .' she thought. 'The Spanish sacrifice.'

'Hurry!' Felipe ordered brusquely. 'They'll send
out a search-party for him and we'll have them on
our heels. There's no time to lose!'

The body of Boucher lay sprawled face down in
the dirt of the yard, the arms thrown out grotesque-
ly, and the head twisted to one side so that Mariana
could see one sightless eye, fixed open in death,
mocking her still. The handle of a throwing-knife
protruded from beneath his shoulder-blade and his
green coat oozed a sticky wetness. Already the
flies, attracted by the smell of fresh blood, were
hovering and buzzing about the corpse.

'Get rid of that!' Felipe said contemptuously,
turning the body with his foot.

The surrounding hills, the farmhouse, everything, swirled about Mariana as she gazed with

horror on the body. She had disliked and distrusted Boucher—but now she would have him for ever on her conscience. She had led him to his death, and, just as surely, she had lured Guy to his.

It was useless to pretend. She had seen the stark and brutal truth in Felipe's face. They would never surrender Guy to the British. They would extract the information they wanted from him by their own hideous methods, and then kill him. His blood would stain her hands: the blood of the man she loved.

Nor was she able any longer to make any pretence about that. She saw it clearly now, in the same reality as she saw the consequences of her treachery. She was no longer physically Guy's prisoner, but though her body was at liberty, her heart was still held fast, a willing captive, his for ever. It had been his since she had first seen him and had known that here was a man like no other she had ever met. How foolish she had been, blind and obstinate, refusing to admit the truth, denying what every instinct, every nerve and muscle of her body, told her.

'Why didn't you make Beaudoin kill me, Guy?' she asked in silent torment. 'It would have been the best thing you could have done for both of us. I have betrayed you, my darling . . . I have betrayed us both.'

She saw Felipe look towards her, the evening breeze blowing back his long hair, emphasising his lean, hawk-like features in all their merciless cruelty.

Deliver . . . from the power of the dog, wrote the Psalmist of old. A dog, indeed. A veritable hound of hell.

CHAPTER
EIGHT

THEY TRAVELLED fast, high up into the hills, putting as much distance as possible between themselves and any possible pursuit. Felipe kept Mariana by him, leaving Guy with the body of his men with whom they had met up. She realised with a sinking heart that this was because Felipe did not wish her to see what they did with their prisoner.

The first night was spent in the open, sleeping on the heather. The cold was intense, eating into Mariana's bones, but it was not that which kept her awake. It was the laughter of the men in the darkness, a short distance away. It was not a happy laughter but a cruel and vicious one, and she knew what caused their mirth.

In the morning, as they set out again, she attempted to plead with Felipe, but he shrugged aside her protests.

'You have a woman's soft heart,' he said indulgently. 'But don't waste your pity on a Frenchman. Forget him.'

'How can I forget when I hear them laughing in that way? Felipe, you promised me—you swore to me you would treat him as a prisoner of war!' she reminded him urgently.

'And kept my word. This *is* how we treat our prisoners of war!' he told her mockingly with his wolfish smile.

'But he already has unhealed injuries which keep him in constant pain!' Mariana cried desperately. 'Your ill-treatment will kill him!'

'He may die,' Felipe conceded with a shrug. 'We are all mortal, so I cannot prevent his dying, eventually.'

'And how long before that happens?'

He shrugged again. 'He's strong, and very obstinate. Besides, I don't want him dead, yet. He can tell us too much.'

'No, Felipe,' she said slowly, shaking her head. 'He will tell you nothing.'

'Leave that to me,' Felipe returned calmly. 'He'll talk.' His deep-set, animal eyes rested on her face. 'Why does it matter so much to you?'

A faint suspicion touched his voice, and Mariana sensed her danger. As evenly as possible, she said, 'It is a matter of honour, Felipe. You, who are a Spanish *hidalgo*, will you do nothing to prevent those—those brutes torturing a helpless man for their devilish amusement?'

'My men have suffered too much from the French!' Felipe was vehement. 'They have seen their villages burned, their women raped, their food and livestock stolen. Don't speak to me of honour! As for the Frenchman, he understands his situation, even if you do not. He knows what to expect.'

'Yes, he has always known,' Mariana said

soberly. 'He told me of the things you'd done, but I refused to believe him.'

'Then, if he knew, he was a fool to allow himself to be trapped!' Felipe caressed her cheek with his fingers. 'A man may hope to be forgiven his sins, Mariana, but not his stupidity!'

'He trusted me,' Mariana said dully.

'As I knew he would,' was Felipe's blunt reply. 'I told you, the French have a fatal vanity regarding women. Faced with a pretty woman, the strongest and most valiant of them is no better than poor Samson in the toils of Delilah! You, my dear, did well. I'm proud of you!' He stroked her cheek again.

'I'm not proud of myself,' Mariana muttered, forcing herself not to flinch before his touch, or before the look in his eyes. They watched her hungrily and, despite her resolve, she stepped back, but too late.

Felipe lunged towards her and she felt herself caught fast in his muscular arms. His long black hair fell across her face as his mouth eagerly sought hers. Mariana thought she would faint. Her senses reeled as she found herself obliged to submit to the fierce passion of his embrace, though it could arouse nothing in her but fear and loathing. There was a savage gleam in his eyes which terrified her, and he drew short, shallow, rasping breaths.

'You know how long I have waited for you!' he panted. 'I have carried in my mind a constant vision of you, as radiant as a solitary star on the blackest of nights. Everything that I have done, everything I have fought for, has been for Spain and for you! Don't criticise what I have done, Mariana. You alone were my inspiration! With every Frenchman killed by me or by my men, I have avenged Miguel's death and the honour of your family. I have washed away the disgrace of Ocaña with French blood. I have fought to be worthy of *you*!'

'No, Felipe!' Mariana protested. 'I never wanted it so!'

'But I have wanted you!' he cried savagely. 'I have dreamed of you, of the touch of your skin and your hair, and the grace of your body. Some men carry images of the saints; I carried you in my heart. It is five years since I told you that, one day, you would be my wife. Do you remember, the night of the ball, in the gardens, by the fountain of Neptune? Now you *are* mine, and nothing will ever part us again!' His hand caressed her shoulder. 'You are modest, and that is right. I should wish any wife of mine to be so. But too much modesty is not needed here. Don't be nervous, it's quiet, no one will come to see what we do,' he whispered. 'My men are occupied with the Frenchman, and we are alone . . .'

Mariana found her voice. 'No, no, Felipe . . . not, not here, not on this hillside, like, like this! Please—later, later . . .' she begged.

Unwillingly he released her. 'Soon,' he promised, 'we shall be together at last.'

When he had gone, Mariana sank down on the heather, her legs no longer able to support her. She was shaking from head to toe, and she rubbed desperately at her mouth as if she could rub away the imprint of his lips. But it was no use. For the moment they were escaping their pursuers, and she was safe. But soon they would be secure in the hills and there would be no need to run, and Felipe would wait no longer to claim his prize.

Mariana stopped shaking as a cold, resolute, acceptance crystallised within her. She herself had brought this about. She had shaped her own destiny. That destiny was to be the wife of Felipe Marquez. It was her fate, and her punishment. But before that happened, she would find the means of righting the terrible wrong she had done the man she loved.

The terrain continued to rise, the incline growing steeper and stonier, the sharp rocks projecting through the thin layer of soil bruising Mariana's feet and causing her to stumble. They crossed a mountain river spilling out of a source somewhere in the High Pyrenees, and tumbling down in an icy torrent. Hill shepherds had built a rough causeway of flat rocks, and on it Mariana crossed, her feet slipping on the wet stones, in terror of falling into the rushing water.

By the second night, Felipe judged they were safe enough to strike a more permanent camp. A fire was lit, and the men set to work cutting down branches to make rough shelters.

Mariana sat on a rock, huddled in her shawl, and watched the man Felipe had ordered to build a shelter for her. He was a sturdy Catalan peasant, good-looking in a coarse fashion despite a pockmarked skin, and he worked quickly and efficiently, slashing at the branches with a large, sharp, bone-handled knife, and whistling to himself as he completed his task.

'Tell me,' Mariana asked him casually. 'Where is the Frenchman?'

The Catalan stopped his work and stared at her, and she wondered if he did not understand her Castilian Spanish. But then he pointed across the clearing.

'There, José guards him.'

At least, Guy was still alive.

Someone shouted from the fire, and the Catalan threw down his knife and went across. He did not come back. The bivouac was more or less finished, and he had forgotten his knife. It lay, gleaming dully, on the ground at Mariana's feet. She picked it up carefully, and wrapped it in her shawl.

Later that evening, Felipe brought her some food to the bivouac. It was a thin watery gazpacho, thickened with oil and bread, and heavily seasoned with cayenne pepper and garlic. It was unspeakably foul. Fortunately, Felipe had not stayed to eat with her, so she was able to pour it away uneaten. On this primitive gazpacho Felipe had subsisted for four years, sustained less by the diet than by his hatred for the French.

Outside, by the fire, the unknown guitarist was playing again. He was a true musician, whoever he was. He was not distracted by his savage surroundings or coarse companions. The music flowed on, sometimes tinkling sweetly, sometimes throbbing

with passion, as if he poured his heart out in his
playing and nothing else mattered to him. Mariana
pulled aside the blanket over the doorway and
peeped out. She could see the men gathered about
the fire, laughing and talking as they ate, and the
slender, youthful silhouette of the guitarist, black
against the orange flames.

Felipe was there, too, deep in conversation with
José. Who, then, guarded the prisoner?

Mariana picked up the Catalan's knife, threw her
shawl over it, and slipped quietly out of the bivouac
and into the shadows. Cautiously she made her way
to the spot the Catalan had indicated to her earlier,
and, trying to make out something in the darkness,
whispered: 'Guy?'

At first she received no reply and ventured to call
his name again, a little more loudly. This time she
was rewarded by a movement to her left and,
groping her way towards it, stumbled upon the
figure of a man, half sitting, half lying, with his back
against a pine-trunk.

Mariana dropped on her knees on the carpet of
pine needles and whispered fearfully, 'Guy, have
they hurt you badly?'

'I'm surprised you didn't come and watch . . .'
the man muttered in a croaking, pain-laden
voice.

'I didn't mean this to happen—' She broke off. It
was useless to protest. He would not believe her.
More urgent matters pressed, anyway. At any
moment, José might return.

'Guy—can you move?'

'I could,' Guy mumbled, 'if I weren't tied hand and foot. What are you doing here, Mariana?' He drew in his breath sharply. 'Does he neglect you?' His voice cracked on a note of mockery.

'I have a knife,' Mariana whispered, ignoring this caustic jibe as best she could. 'Hold still, Guy, and I'll cut the rope round your wrists.'

'Why are you doing this?' he demanded hoarsely, as she sawed awkwardly with the knife. 'What are you playing at now?'

'I'm giving you a chance to escape!' she retorted.

'Having gone to such trouble to get me here, why do that?' His voice reflected his disbelief.

'Because Felipe lied to me! He promised to take you to the British, and now I know he means to keep you here and kill you. There!' The rope parted.

Guy flexed his cramped arms and rubbed his raw wrists. 'Give me the knife,' he ordered breathlessly. 'Be quick!'

She handed it to him and he leaned forward with a grunt and cut through the rope which secured his feet.

'Go on, Guy!' she begged urgently. 'Get away from here. Hurry! Ah!'

Her voice stopped on a choked cry as she felt the cold sharp tip of the knife touch her throat.

'You, too, *querida*,' his voice, filled with an ice-cold menace, breathed into her ear. 'Don't start screaming now, or I shall be obliged to cut your pretty throat!'

'Are you mad? What are you doing? I can't come

with you, why should you want me?' she stammered.

'Because I've learned the hard way that I can't trust you, *querida*, unless I can see you!'

He struggled to his feet, drawing deep pain-wracked breaths, and braced himself with his hand against the pine-tree.

'And because I need you as a hostage as never before. If your lover there catches me, he will tear me slowly into little pieces. But I saw how he looked at you. *You* he certainly wants all of a piece! While you're with me, he'll hesitate . . .' He grasped her arm roughly. 'Go on, move!'

With Guy pushing her ahead of him, they stumbled across the carpet of needles which muffled their steps, and began to slither and slide down the barren hillside in the darkness.

Guy pulled Mariana along with him, forcing her to keep up a breakneck pace through a night riddled with unseen obstacles. Panting for breath and suffering an agonising stitch in her side, Mariana struggled across the rough terrain.

'Guy, I can't keep this up!' she managed to gasp.

'You can,' he panted, 'and you will! If I can, so can you!'

The escape must surely have been discovered by now, Mariana thought as they plunged on downwards in their reckless course. Her heart throbbed as if it would burst, and every gasping breath rent her lungs with a searing pain.

But Guy did not stop until they reached the bottom of the slope and there, mercifully, he paused and hissed, 'Listen!'

Slowly the blood stopped pounding in Mariana's ears. The night air stirred the pine-tops, and very faintly on the scented breeze was carried the sound of distant shouting.

'The hunt is on!' Guy said grimly. 'Come on!'

'How do you know which way to go?' she asked, bewildered.

'I've kept my eye on the sun and the stars. We are going back the way we came.'

Indeed they were, for eventually they heard the sound of water and reached the mountain river. But unable to locate the causeway in the darkness, they were forced to plunge into it, the icy water numbing Mariana's limbs.

As it rose to her breast she began to be afraid, clutching at Guy's arm. Then, suddenly, she slipped and fell forward, the clear, cold water closing over her head for a moment of swirling terror, until a strong hand hauled her, choking and spluttering, above the surface again.

'Hold tight!' he urged her. 'We're there!'

He dragged her out on to the further bank, and they set off again. Her sodden skirts wrapped themselves about her ankles, threatening to bring her down, and tears of exhaustion and fear ran down Mariana's face.

'Let me go, Guy. Please, leave me here!' she begged.

'No!' he returned viciously. 'Let you point the way to your friends? We stay together, you and I!'

At last, as the grey streaks of dawn began to lighten the sky, they came upon a deserted turf-roofed shepherd's hut.

'Here,' Guy muttered, and she realised that he, too, was exhausted. 'We'll rest till it's light.'

They both stumbled into the hut and collapsed on the earthen floor. Mariana thought she was going to die. The blood roared in her head and every muscle of her body ached. Pillowing her head on her folded arms, she allowed a welcome blackness to engulf her.

Someone was shaking her shoulder. Mariana swam to the surface through a sea of unconsciousness, flickering her eyelids and moaning. Light came from somewhere, and birdsong. Someone bent over her, and she felt something brush her forehead lightly, warm, gentle and soft, like a kiss. Slowly she opened her eyes and focused them on the face above hers.

'Guy?' she whispered.

His face receded. 'Get up!' his voice ordered.

She struggled to a sitting position and stared at him in confusion. Now that it was light, she saw him for the first time since his capture, his face swollen and bruised from the beatings he had received, and smeared with dried blood.

'We have to go on,' he said harshly. 'Can you go on, Mariana?'

'Yes—yes, I think so.'

'Good!' He turned and set off without waiting for her or looking back to see if she followed.

Mariana scrambled to her feet and stumbled after him.

'Where are we going?' she asked breathlessly, trying to keep up as he strode out.

'Back to the house.'

'Back? But I thought you'd try to reach the French border!'

'The White Wolf will think that, too, I hope. Besides, you forget—I'm responsible for a squadron of cavalry. I can't just abandon them,' he said grimly. 'Come on, give me your hand. It won't be so bad; every step we get nearer to what passes here for civilisation makes it more difficult for them to follow us. If we reach the high road, we are safe.'

Obediently, she gave him her hand. He grasped it firmly and they set off across the heather and bracken. The sun shone warmly on their bodies, drying their damp clothing, and a lark sang high in the blue sky above them.

For a long time they travelled in silence until Mariana, unable to bear it any longer, asked in a small, weary voice, 'You despise me, Guy, don't you? You must hate me very much. I understand. I can only expect you to.'

'I overlooked your bigoted little mind!' Guy replied brusquely, quickening his pace. 'When I tried to force my drunken attentions on you, I should have known you would take your revenge!'

'No, Guy, it wasn't because of what you did that evening!' Mariana cried. 'At least, don't think that!' Stumbling alongside him, unable to match his long strides, she continued with difficulty, 'Please let me try and explain!'

He did not reply, but stared expressionlessly into the distance ahead as if he were indifferent to her words.

'Felipe persuaded me to do it,' Mariana went on desperately, aware of the futility of trying to explain her motives to him. 'Guy, please don't go so fast, and at least listen! Felipe talked about Spain, and about Miguel, my brother, and he—he made it into a kind of a test to see if I loved him. He made use of me and he lied to me. Whatever my reasons, what I did was wrong, but I believed he would take you to the British! So you see, it wasn't because of anything *you* did. Perhaps I did choose that moment, because you were drunk and I thought you would—' she faltered. 'But it wasn't the reason! It doesn't make me proud of myself, Guy, to tell you any of this,' she concluded miserably.

When he still did not answer or show any sign of even having heard, Mariana felt a flicker of resentment, and added with a touch of her former spirit, 'I've got a pain in my side, and if you won't slow down, I shall just sit down in the heather, and you'll have to carry me, if you want to take me with you!'

Guy halted so suddenly that she cannoned into him with a gasp.

'You are not proud of what you did?' he said fiercely. 'Do you think I am proud of myself, Mariana? I let myself be trapped by the oldest decoy ever used—a pretty face! Look at me, and you'll see a man whose stupidity could deservedly have cost him his life, and did cost one man his!'

He set off again across the rough terrain, though this time a little more slowly.

'Guy, don't blame yourself,' Mariana begged. 'It was all my doing, all of it! I'm sorry about Boucher. I didn't like him, but I would never have led him deliberately to his death! And I wouldn't have led you to Felipe if I had known what they would do to you. I begged Felipe to stop them hurting you,' she continued wretchedly. 'I could hear them laughing. It was horrible, horrible! Those men are not patriots, they are fiends!'

Her agony and misery echoed in her voice with such painful sincerity that it seemed at last to make some impression on him.

'It takes more than a little rough treatment to finish off an old *grognard* like me, *querida*,' he said. 'At different times in my career I've been shot, bayoneted, felled by cannon and slashed by sabre, ridden over by cavalry and blasted by English shrapnel—and here I am, as you can see, still alive! I'm no beauty, I grant you! Not with half a face, broken nose, broken ribs, more scars than I can count and, to top it all, I lost a couple of teeth to your friend, José! However, I've two arms, two legs and I'm at liberty . . . and the sun is shining!' he added unexpectedly.

He glanced at her, his split, swollen lips twisted briefly into his lop-sided grin.

'You are a brave man,' Mariana said soberly.

'Don't muddle up your heroes, Marianne!' he

retorted. 'I'm the enemy, remember? The Patriotic Hero—your lover—is behind us somewhere, breathing revenge on me, and lust for you!'

Mariana flushed and was silenced.

In the evening they came across some late-fruiting blueberry bushes and sat down to share their find. Mariana realised for the first time just how long she had been without food, and how hungry she was. She even regretted, now, that she had not eaten the gazpacho.

'How do you like living as a gipsy?' Guy asked her, surveying her torn, dirty dress and mud-streaked face. He picked a piece of bracken out of her hair. With the last mile or two, his manner had become more relaxed, though he still glanced back regularly.

'Not very much,' Mariana confessed. 'I wish we had something else to eat. I'm still hungry.'

'That will pass off,' he said. 'The body adjusts. A man adjusts to anything, provided he has the will to live.'

The will to live. He had kept that throughout his turbulent career. He had seen more death, more suffering, more massacres that she could possibly imagine. But her betrayal was something different, a personal treachery of a special kind. Nevertheless, even that he had somehow survived.

Guy glanced about them. 'We'll get some sleep here. It's as good a place as any. If we set out again at first light, we'll be at the house soon after breakfast time.'

He threw himself back on the heather and looked up at her.

'Here,' he stretched out his arm towards her. 'Come and lie down by me. It's all right,' he added drily, seeing her apprehensive face. 'It's for the sake of mutual warmth. There's no reason why either of us should seek pneumonia. I swear, the condition I'm in, I couldn't do anything likely to offend you, even if I wished to!'

Mariana lay down cautiously beside him in the crook of his arm.

'You'll have to imagine I'm he . . .' he muttered, and, closing his eyes, fell promptly asleep.

The sun was sinking below the horizon, fire-red fingers playing across the sky and lending a rosy glow to his features. He looked as peaceful as a child. As the twilight closed in on them, Mariana put her head on his shoulder, sensing his deep, even breathing and absorbing the warmth of his body. She closed her own eyes, weariness overtaking her, and slept beside him.

The moon came up and cast a cold, silver light over the hillside, on which the patches of black shadow lurked, and familiar shapes became strange and threatening. The sudden flapping of wings as a night bird flew across the sky alone broke the stillness.

Mariana dreamed, a confusing and deeply disturbing dream in which the ceiling of the painted bedroom revolved slowly like a great wheel of Fortune. The naked figures of Cupid and Psyche and the cherubs swirled about until they became confused, a jumble of pink bodies, arms and legs, rose garlands, pouting lips and gauze draperies, merging at last into two quite different naked bodies lying on the bed below, belonging to people she felt she should know, but whom, with the elusiveness of the dream world, she could not at first identify. And then she saw their faces, and knew them at last . . .

She awoke suddenly with a little cry. For a moment the confusion of the dream world lingered and she could not recall where she was, and wondered why the bed was now so hard and what had happened to the satin sheet. Then the confusion was dispelled and she remembered.

Beside her, Guy stirred, muttering also to himself in his sleep, as if he too dreamed, and she wondered if it was of Lisette. Fearing she had disturbed him, she lay as still as she could, watching the moon and the scudding clouds above.

There was a sudden rush of wings and a shrill squeak. A grotesque black shape flew up out of the undergrowth and winged its way towards a clump of trees—an owl, bearing its tiny prey still wriggling helplessly in the hunter's grip.

Mariana shivered and nestled automatically closer to her companion. He tossed restlessly, turning his head towards her so that his lips touched her ear, and murmured again in that unintelligible way of sleepers. The words sounded French, but she could not make them out. His breath tickled her ear-lobe. Suddenly he rolled over towards her and threw his arm and shoulder across her body, so that his head rested against her breast. Mariana curled her arm protectively about his head and stroked his cropped hair tenderly with the tips of her fingers.

She had denied this man her bed. In reality, the lovers of the dream fantasy could never be. But she shared with him now this patch of purple heather beneath the stars, and, for this brief moment, he lay sleeping in her arms, and was hers.

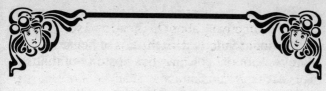

CHAPTER
NINE

IT WAS very early when she awoke again, and Guy still slept motionless beside her, one arm flung up under his head. She lay for a while, the warm early morning sun bathing her face, and studied that scarred, Roman-nosed, unshaven and bruised profile, knowing that, for her at least, nothing could improve on it, and it would always be the most handsome face of all. Then she slipped gently out from beneath his other, encircling, arm and sat up on the heather.

As she did, she experienced again that strange and unpleasant tingling of the nerves she had felt before the farmhouse. Someone was watching them. Someone very near.

Mariana turned slowly.

He was about five yards away, sitting on an outcropping stony bank, very still and silent, his sunburned hawk-like features in their frame of tangled black hair immovable, and only the deepset animal eyes, fixed on them, alive with a venomous intelligence.

'How long have you been there, Felipe?' she whispered through lips paralysed by fear.

'Since sunrise,' he said. 'When I found you—in his arms.'

'It's not as you think, Felipe,' she began, but fell silent before the cold, vicious hostility of that savage gaze.

'We did not know where to search,' he said, 'and I asked myself what the Frenchman would do. If he were sensible, he would head for the High Pyrenees and the French frontier. But he has not much sense, your Frenchman. He has a mule-headed obstinacy and an ability to withstand pain which might almost be called courage. But he has not much sense. He will attempt to find his men, I reasoned to myself. He will go back the way we came. I was right.'

'Your men . . . ?'

'I am alone,' Felipe replied. 'You thought you had outdistanced me, but you forgot, the wolf hunts by night. While you slept—with him—I followed your trail to this place.'

Beside her, Guy's breathing seemed to change its pattern, but he did not open his eyes or stir.

'The pig sleeps,' Felipe said contemptuously. 'It is fortunate I alone found you, Mariana. I would not have wished any man of mine to see a Spanish woman debase herself so,' his voice sank to a hiss, 'to lie with a Frenchman.'

'No, Felipe . . .' Mariana shook her head desperately. 'You're wrong!'

'Go and sit over there,' he ordered, pointing a little way away. 'Don't touch him!' This, as she made to wake Guy.

'What are you going to do?' she faltered, terrified.

'Get over there,' he snarled, 'and watch! The Frenchman will dishonour no more Spanish women—or any woman!'

Mariana crept stumbling towards the place he indicated and crouched huddled on the earth.

Felipe stood up and walked over to Guy's recumbent form, looking down at the Frenchman with an expression of indescribable ferocity.

Suddenly Guy's still body came to life. Mariana shrieked, and Felipe uttered an oath as his feet were jerked from under him. The two men, locked in a life or death struggle, slithered down the hillside, each seeking the second of advantage which would deliver his foe to him.

Mariana scrambled to her feet and watched, horrified and powerless, as to her dismay she saw Felipe throw his long arms around Guy's injured ribs in a slowly closing bear-hug. Guy's face, white and twisted in agony, turned towards her.

She looked round wildly and saw a large stone near by. Without reflecting, she snatched it up and ran towards the fighting men, the stone raised to strike. But before she reached them, Felipe's grip suddenly slackened, the lean cheeks drew back in a mirthless grin, and the deepset eyes, staring up at her, glazed.

Guy drew a deep shuddering breath and thrust the guerrilla leader away from him. Felipe fell back, spreadeagled in the heather, the bone hilt of the Catalan's knife protruding from his chest, blood slowly seeping across his shirt.

Mariana dropped the stone and fell on her knees beside his motionless body. When she looked up, she saw Guy staring at her, an odd expression on his face.

'I have killed him!' he said hoarsely.

'I . . . I thought he would kill you,' she whispered.

Guy shook his head, panting, and running his tongue over his lips. He staggered to his feet, and Mariana grabbed his arm to steady him.

He shook her off. 'You were too late,' he said with difficulty, his hand clasped to his injured side. 'You were too late to dash my brains out, and save him.'

'No!' she cried. 'You're wrong, I meant to strike *him*!'

But Guy seized her arm. 'Come on!' he ordered roughly, and set off across the heather, dragging her with him.

They reached the great house later than Guy had hoped, just before noon. It stood, deceptively peaceful amongst the greenery of its gardens, its shutters tightly fastened. Only a few crows in a nearby tree, flapping away, cawing loudly at their approach, signalled their arrival to anyone watching.

'I thought we should never get here,' Mariana gasped through parched lips. 'I couldn't go another step.'

'Wait!' Guy touched her arm and she looked up

to see his eyes narrowed suspiciously as he surveyed the mansion before them. 'Something's wrong. No one on guard.'

'It's noon, everyone takes a siesta at noon,' she protested.

'Not in the Grand Army, *querida*,' he retorted. 'Some poor devil always has sentry duty, especially here in hostile territory.'

'There's someone!' Mariana pointed as a woman's figure emerged from the house. 'It's Juana. Juana!' she cried out, before Guy could prevent her. 'Juana, we've come back!'

The woman gave a shriek and came running to meet them, gesticulating wildly.

'May the saints preserve us! Dear lady, you look more dead than alive! Come inside quickly, and the Frenchman too.'

'Where are my men?' Guy demanded, seizing the maid by the wrist.

'Why, gone, señor!' Juana exclaimed round-eyed, and staring at him as though he were a ghost.

'Gone?'

'Juana, what's happened?' Mariana asked urgently.

'Happened? Everything's happened. I couldn't begin to tell it all out here. Señor, you can't keep my lady out here when she's fainting on her feet! Only look at the state she's in! Come inside. There is no one there, no one at all.'

She urged them ahead of her into the house and they were able to see for themselves that it was indeed quite empty. Not so much as a harness-buckle remained to mark the presence of the dragoons—only the ruined furniture and fittings and a strange emptiness caused by the removal of all valuable objects bore silent witness to the passage of the French.

Guy collapsed into a chair and said wearily, 'Tell me . . .'

'Why, señor, after you failed to come back with my lady, having gone to meet that rogue José—who is my cousin's cousin, I regret to say, and never was any good, even as a child. I remember—'

'Juana, please!' Mariana cried. 'What happened?'

'Well, Doña Mariana, they sent out a search party for you, and found the body of the one who was killed.' Juana paused to cross herself piously. 'Then they questioned the old woman at the farm, and she was frightened and told them everything. How Don Felipe sent a child on a donkey along the road to watch for you, and come and tell him when you were near—'

Guy struck his forehead in a gesture of despair, and groaned, 'I should have known!'

'How Don Felipe and José had captured you, señor, and taken you and my lady up into the hills. They searched, of course, but it was late, and grew dark. At dawn they searched again, and found nothing. Then, towards noon, there came other dragoons—'

'Other?' Guy demanded.

'Yes, señor. A whole company with other officers. They looked very grave when they were told what had happened. The leader of them said that you were surely dead. *"Mort, mort!"* I heard him say, and I know that means "dead". Indeed, we did all think you must be dead, for the White Wolf keeps no prisoners, everyone knows that.'

Juana broke off to stare suspiciously at Guy, as though he might somehow be faking life.

'Go on,' he said in a tired voice.

'So the senior officer said—he was a very fine looking man, not young, with white moustaches, but sat very straight on his horse—he said they could do nothing for you now, and must move on. So they did, and took your men with them, as he said they were under his command now.' Juana shook her head so that her gold loop earrings swung. 'That sergeant didn't want to go. *"Pas sans lui, pas sans lui!"* he kept shouting.' Juana repeated the French syllables as she had heard them, with strong Spanish overtones. 'Whatever that means,' she added.

'It means "not without him",' Guy told her with a sigh. 'Poor Beaudoin. He would always be the last to desert me.'

'In the end they had to drag him away,' Juana declared. 'But they all went off, and I don't know where.'

'Guy, I'm sorry,' Mariana ventured to put her hand on his sleeve. 'What will you do now?'

'I don't mean to sit around here till either your Spanish patriots or the British arrive!' he exclaimed. 'I shall make my own way to France!' He pulled his arm away from her roughly. 'And get your hand off me!' he almost snarled at her, getting to his feet and stumbling away from her.

Rebuffed, Mariana flushed. 'You can't go anywhere, Guy. You're exhausted. You haven't eaten, you're in pain—'

'I'm still free!' he interrupted her harshly. 'Nothing else matters!'

Mariana looked away, feeling the tears sting her eyelids.

'If you are hungry, there are some eggs!' said Juana cheerfully. 'I hid them away from the soldiers. I'll fry them now, and you and my lady can eat. What *you* need, señor, is some hot water to clean yourself up! Bless us, but you look as though a whole herd of fighting bulls had been driven over you!'

'I'll help you—' Mariana began, but he gestured her aside impatiently.

'I don't need your help. I can manage!'

'No, you can't!' she protested. 'Guy, those injured ribs need strapping up and you can't do it yourself! I understand how you feel about me, but you are going to have to let me help you. Here, take off your coat. I'll go and see if there are any sheets left to make into bandages.'

He muttered under his breath, but submitted impatiently to her ministrations. Mariana was horrified at the number of new bruises which bore witness to the treatment he had received at the hands of the *guerrilleros*. She tried not to hurt him further as she unwound the soiled linen strips about his chest and ribcage, but the wound was well and truly broken open now, swollen, and weeping an angry mixture of blood and pus. In response to his colourfully expressed instructions, she cleaned the whole unpleasant mess away with vinegar from the kitchen before bandaging it afresh.

'And don't expect me to apologise for my language!' he added aggressively, as he staggered to his feet and tipped the contents of a bowl of water over his head, still cursing to himself and shaking his cropped head like a terrier.

Mariana remembered the first time she had ever seen him properly, looking very much like this, with the shining rivulets of water running over his bronzed, muscular body.

'He is strong,' she thought. 'Strong in body, strong in spirit, and strong in his hatred. He could be a Spaniard. He will never forgive me.'

Juana brought the eggs, deep-fried in oil so that they puffed up in golden envelopes, crackling and crisp. When they had eaten, Mariana ventured to mention his plan of making his own way to France.

'You will need a horse, Guy.'

'Why not say I need wings?' he returned ungraciously. 'It's just as impossible I could get a horse as those!'

'Perhaps not,' Mariana said slowly.

'Pah! Everything on four legs which wasn't swaybacked and broken-kneed was taken long ago! I know, I've scoured the countryside for army remounts. Horses drop like flies in this confounded climate!'

'If I could get you a horse—' she began.

'As you could get me the White Wolf? What ingenious plan have you in mind now, I wonder?' he taunted.

'It's no use speaking like that!' Mariana's Spanish temper rose to the boil. 'I know you don't trust me. Hate me as much as you like, but without a horse you'll never even leave this district, let alone reach France! And only I can get you one.'

'Where?' he countered, but he was listening closely.

Juana, who had come into the room and stood, arms folded, by the door, interpolated, 'Doña Eugenia.'

'That's right,' Mariana said.

'Perhaps you'd like to explain?' Guy suggested icily.

'Of course. Doña Eugenia is my godmother. She's very elderly and very rich, and a little, a little . . . eccentric. You see, her husband died over twenty years ago. She loved him very much, and it affected her.'

'You're trying to say the old lady is quite mad?' he enquired.

'No! Only a little odd. Everything is kept as it was when her husband was alive. There is a pack of hounds in the kennels which never hunts, and saddle-horses in the stables which are only ridden out for exercise by their grooms. They are there because her husband would have kept them, do you understand?'

'No, but I've long since ceased to understand anything emanating from you. All right. So this crazy old woman has a stable full of horses. Will she part with any?'

'She's always been fond of me. There's a chance. I'll go and ask her.'

'All right,' he agreed. 'Go and ask her. Your maid here stays with me, and if you come back with a crowd of your Spanish patriots, she will be the first victim of your treachery, do you understand?'

'You don't need to threaten me, Guy, I don't mean to betray you,' Mariana said quietly.

'Then bring two horses, one for me, and one for you!' His order was brusque. 'You're coming with me as far as the frontier. After that, I don't care what you do. But I'm not leaving you here to go running to the British as soon as I've ridden out.'

'You will be the death of my lady!' wailed Juana protestingly.

'My intention,' he said, in his dry way, 'is that she won't be the death of me!'

'Come in, child, come in! Don't fidget about back there in the shadows. Come closer, where I can see you.'

The huge room, furnished with massive pieces of furniture ornately carved from wood hewn in the forests of South America, was visible only by the light from a partly curtained window. Mariana walked carefully across the polished floor.

Her godmother watched her with her sharp, hooded eyes. She resembled, Mariana thought, nothing so much as a little black crow. Dressed from head to toe in the heavy mourning she had donned the day her husband had died, twenty years before, only the glitter of her jet earrings and necklaces in the poor light matched the glitter of her eyes, themselves like two jet beads. She wore a black lace veil, and an old-fashioned gown with a bodice stiffened with whalebone, and a hooped skirt such as had been fashionable in her youth. A thin heavily beringed hand, wizened and dry as if mummified, stretched out and gripped Mariana's wrist with surprising strength.

'Well?' croaked her godmother harshly.

'How are you, Godmother?' Mariana ventured.

'How am I? I am old and I am ugly! Don't ask stupid questions. Sit down, child, here, by me, on that little stool.'

All of this was delivered not in malice or anger, but with a touch of cynical humour. Mariana sat down by the old lady, who stroked her god-daughter's smooth cheek with the tips of her fingers. It was a touch like the brush of falling autumn leaves.

'Pretty!' she muttered. 'And virtuous, I suppose? Well? Do you sleep alone, eh?'

'I did not think *you* would ask me that!' Mariana objected resentfully.

'Why not? Think I've forgotten what goes or between a man and a woman, eh? Well, don't look so shocked! Tell me what you want. When young people take it into their heads to visit old ones, without being summoned, it is because they want something.'

'You are unfair, Godmother!' Mariana replied. 'I've visited you often, and never asked for anything!' She blushed. 'But you are right this time,' she admitted. 'I have come to beg a favour.'

'Then ask it, child. Don't make a long speech of it. What is it you want?' The sharp little eyes bored into Mariana's face as Doña Eugenia leaned forward with a rustle of black silk.

Hesitantly, Mariana explained her immediate need of two saddle-horses.

'Two? For what purpose? Where are you going?' demanded the old lady. 'Speak up!'

'I can't tell you, Godmother. Please don't refuse me,' Mariana begged.

'Two . . .' repeated the old lady to herself. 'Two horses. An elopement, eh? Is that it? Well?'

'I . . . not exactly. But something like that, Godmother,' Mariana said cautiously, knowing the old woman's obsession with affairs of the heart.

'Who?' Doña Eugenia leaned so far forward that her face was pushed right into Mariana's. 'Who is he? Not that devil Felipe Marquez?'

'No!' Mariana exclaimed, startled and a little dismayed. 'Not him, I swear!'

'I am glad,' said her godmother. 'He's a bad lot. Always was. Now I hear they make a hero of him. But I've known him from a child, and his father before him. Bad blood breeds bad blood. There are men who know only how to destroy. Felipe Marquez is such a man.'

'The war . . .' Mariana ventured.

'Pah! War? Such men do not need a war. They

know only how to destroy, it is bred in them. Even when they love,' she leaned forward and hissed, 'they are destroyers!'

'Felipe is dead,' Mariana said quietly.

'Hah!' The old lady raised her eyebrows. 'Who killed him?'

'What makes you think he was killed?' Mariana attempted to evade her godmother's direct gaze.

'Because men such as that do not die peacefully in their beds with a priest at the pillows!' Doña Eugenia said with a snort. 'This lover of yours, did he kill him? Was it a duel?'

'A—a sort of duel,' Mariana admitted. 'He is a Frenchman, Godmother.'

'Is he? Then I'm not surprised you come to me with such secrecy!' Her godmother paused and shook her head as if to clear her mind. 'I'm old,' she went on. She sounded tired.

Mariana looked at her in alarm, fearing the old lady was about to wander and had forgotten the preceding conversation.

'I am old,' Doña Eugenia repeated, 'but I remember. My husband was a fine man. But my family did not like him. He bribed my maid to pass me his love-letters during Mass. I hid the letters in my bodice,' she tapped her bosom. 'He was a handsome man, a fine, strong man . . . he often told me, he envied his letters their place!' She gave a sudden cackle of laughter.

'I told my father that I would marry no one but Carlos or go into a convent. My poor father wept because I was a favourite daughter, but in the end

he consented. Afterwards, Carlos told me that on
our wedding-day, as we left the church, my father
took him aside and said, "My boy, I now consider
you my son. But if you mistreat my daughter, or
break her heart, I will have you killed. You have
my word on it."'

She stared hard at Mariana. 'Where are the men
in your family to protect you? I know. They are
dead! If this fine French lover of yours deserts you,
it will do no good to run to me! Well, if a woman
wants a man, she must learn to hold on to him. You
shall have your horses.'

'I—I thank you, Doña Eugenia!' Mariana
embraced the old lady.

'You want money, too, I suppose,' Doña
Eugenia said sourly, though not displeased.
'Don't mumble. You will need money. Go to the
drawer in the desk over there,' she pointed into the
gloom.

Mariana did as bid and brought back a leather
wallet.

'Keep it.' Doña Eugenia pushed it away as
Mariana made to hand it to her. 'And call Julio, so I
may send him down to the stable for your two
horses. And remember! If a woman loses a man,
she has only herself to blame! Make him want
you!'

'Yes, Godmother,' Mariana said quietly.

Guy came out on to the terrace as they rode up, but
said nothing until the groom had left. Then he came
slowly down the steps and walked round the two

horses, a peculiar expression on his face.

'They are all right, aren't they?' Mariana asked anxiously.

'All right?' He looked up. 'These are Andalusian thoroughbreds! On my pay I couldn't buy a horse like this unless I sold everything else except the clothes I stood up in!' He reached up and patted the glossy neck of the nearer horse which was dancing nervously, tossing its long, flowing mane. 'Easy, my beauty, steady!' He walked away a little and stared morosely at the two animals. 'Do you know what a horse like that is worth, Mariana?' he asked quietly.

'You've just told me, a great deal of money.'

'Money? I'm not speaking of money now. A horse like that is worth a cavalryman's life! I have seen the English cavalry ride down ours, not because they were better soldiers but because they were better mounted! Men's lives lost needlessly because the wretched beasts they rode were simply bowled over by the impact of a charging cavalry horse of the first mettle, like this!' He pointed to the nearer horse again and with his voice growing louder and more angry, demanded, 'And you tell me that half-mad old woman has a stableful of these animals, doing nothing? And I have led men into battle on—' He broke off and turned on his heel, away from her.

'I'm sorry, Guy,' Mariana faltered, unable to think of anything else she could say to him, and feeling hopelessly inadequate in the face of the evident deep emotion he felt.

He shrugged. 'No matter—now. Get ready. We're leaving.'

'Guy,' Mariana urged. 'You can't go out of here in uniform! We can surely find you some clothes.'

'Well, well,' he said drily. 'You really mean to get me shot, or—more likely if I'm captured out of uniform—hung for a spy!'

'I forgot that,' Mariana admitted dismally. 'Then we shall have to find you a cloak, something to cover the uniform up.'

'There are a man's clothes upstairs, Doña Mariana,' Juana offered. 'They belong to the Duke. Though everyone knows he lives with his mistress in Seville and seldom ever comes here. He doesn't get on with his wife, because she—'

'Then he won't need his cloak,' Guy interrupted firmly. 'Go and find it, Juana.'

'How long will it take us to reach the Pyrenees?' Mariana asked.

'The Pyrenees? By tomorrow evening, if we push on. To cross the frontier . . .' he fell silent.

To cross the frontier—at this time an almost impossible task, as they both knew only too well.

CHAPTER
TEN

AT FIRST the high road was almost deserted. It stretched ahead of them, stony and dusty. Occasionally they passed a solitary peasant with a creaking bullock cart, and once a line of black-clad women carrying bundles of washing on their heads down to the river. Some of them glanced curiously at the two riders, the young girl and the man well wrapped in a cloak.

They had been travelling for about an hour when they saw ahead of them a moving cloud of dust.

'A large party ahead,' Guy pointed. 'Troops of some kind.'

'What shall we do?' Mariana asked.

He scowled in thought. 'We'll leave this road and cut a parallel course over open country. It won't slow us up that much. Your Spanish roads seem more designed to hinder travellers than help them.'

He turned his horse's head and she followed him into the scrub-dotted countryside. They followed the same direction as before, keeping about half a mile from the high road. They seemed to be drawing level with the cloud of dust, which seemed now to be stationary, whatever caused it having stopped to rest.

'We'll go a little nearer,' Guy said, 'in case they are ours. But stay by me.'

As they approached, the dust cloud thinned, and they could see that a fairly large body of troops had halted by the roadside. Some of them appeared to be eating.

'Guy!' Mariana cried excitedly. 'They're wearing blue coats! They're French!'

'Yes, yes,' he agreed doubtfully. 'But we'll approach slowly, all the same. Their sentries may be nervous and likely to shoot any stranger who rides up to their camp.'

They began to make their way cautiously down a rocky defile towards the road when suddenly, from behind them, they heard a jingle of harness and the thud of hoofs.

Guy snatched at the reins of Mariana's horse and urged them both behind an outcrop of rock shaded by stunted trees. He jumped to the ground and dragged her down out of the saddle with scant ceremony.

'Hold your horse's nostrils, like this!' he hissed, clamping his hand across his own beast's muzzle to prevent it whinnying.

They were only just in time. A small party of blue-coated riders burst out of the defile behind them, driving along between them several horses they had apparently taken down to the river to water.

As they passed, one shouted to his companions, *'Macht schnell!'*

'Damn!' Guy breathed. 'They're not French!

They're Hussars of the King's German Legion!'

'Which king?' asked Mariana, bewildered.

'George of England, of course! Hanoverians in British service. Wait!' He signalled her urgently to silence and grasped her arm to warn her.

Someone else was coming along the track. Two more riders came into view, ambling sedately along and laughing together. As they drew near to the hidden Mariana and Guy, one reined up and called out to his companion, '*Warte mal!*'

He fished a clay pipe out of his pocket and began placidly to fill it.

Mariana's horse threw up its head and it was only with difficulty that she was able to keep it quiet.

The Hanoverian was having little success in lighting his pipe. Mariana began to fear he would never move on, and felt a little trickle of perspiration run down her brow. At last, with several muttered oaths, he gave it up as a bad job and rode on at a trot after his companion.

'They've gone!' Mariana whispered.

Guy's grey eyes were resting on her thoughtfully. 'You could have called out to him,' he said quietly. 'Why didn't you?'

'I told you,' she said emotionally. 'I betrayed you once—but I won't betray you again!'

He seemed to hesitate, then said grimly, 'Let's get out of here. One close call is enough!'

They set off away from the camping German troops and resumed their original course after a safe distance. But Mariana could not dismiss this evidence of the British advance so lightly from her mind.

'Those Germans,' she said now. 'Does that mean that the British are very close?'

'It might do.' Guy glanced at her a little sardonically. 'Why? Do you hope to be rescued by a dashing sortie of scarlet coats?'

'If I didn't call out to the Hanoverian, then you should know I don't!' Mariana riposted.

'I would be a fool to believe I knew anything about you,' he replied coolly. 'I made that mistake before.'

'I've tried to explain to you,' Mariana said hopelessly. 'You don't understand, and you won't try.'

'I'm a simple soldier,' he retorted. 'Before I met you, I fought when I was ordered, took my pleasures where I found them, and made love where love was offered. My motives were honest, if not always entirely honourable. Now you, *querida*, seem inspired by a set of motives which are somehow to be considered honourable, but to me appear somewhat dishonest. Forgive me, but I find this confusing.'

'If my motives are complicated, it's because life is complicated,' Mariana replied with a sigh.

'Señorita, you spoke to me once of Ocaña. Well, I played my part in that engagement, and I can't say I particularly enjoyed any of it. However, it held one advantage over my dealings with you. I knew where I was, and I knew where the enemy was—and he fought in a way I understood. But you and I are fighting different kinds of war, Mariana.'

'Guy, what was it like at Ocaña? Tell me about it,' she asked impulsively.

He hunched his shoulders. 'What do you want me to say? The Spanish thought they had us trapped. They expected it to be another Baylen. So confident was their command that they installed themselves comfortably at an upstairs window, with a case of wine, to view the rout of the French!' He gave a short laugh. 'Imagine the horror of the poor Spanish general when, instead of jubilant Spaniards, he saw us, French dragoons, dashing up to his door. It was like a theatrical farce. We burst in at the front, like the outraged husband, and he and his staff leapt out at the back like the escaping lover! We almost caught a fine fish, but he just slipped through the net.'

The horses trotted on a little way, and then slowed to a walk as the ground grew more uneven.

'The aftermath of a battle is always worse than the action itself,' Guy said quietly. 'That is when you gather up the debris, human and otherwise. There was a monastery near there, only a small place. It had sustained several direct hits, but none the less somehow remained for the most part intact. As the smoke and dust were settling, I saw a most odd sight coming towards me through the haze. It was a monk, clutching at his skirts like an old lady, and stumbling over the rubble and the holes in the ground. He kept shouting out that he sought a French officer, so I called him over.

'He came up, trembling like a leaf and more than

half convinced I would cut his head off. The reputation of the Mamelukes casts its shadow over us all! Anyway, he'd come to beg protection for the Spanish wounded whom he and his brother monks had carried to their church. He took me there, to show me that they were men genuinely too injured to fight and that there were no able-bodied escapers hiding amongst them.

'The church was not large, but it was the worst place I have ever seen, and I've seen a few ambulance-stations and none of them was pretty! That place was full of shrieking men with smashed limbs and gaping wounds. The straw underfoot was so slippery with blood I could hardly keep my feet on it, and the stench so appalling I could scarcely draw breath, nor did I want to breathe air so foul. The flies clustered about the wounded so gorged with blood that they could no longer take wing, and you could gather them up with your hand.'

Guy stared unseeingly into the distance, as his mind relived that memory.

'There was one youngster I remember who lay by the door, dying and unable to move for fearful injuries, but quite conscious. He saw my French uniform and, as I passed, he called out to me in French and begged that I would finish him off, a *coup de grâce* to spare him his agony.'

'Did you do it?' Mariana whispered in horror.

He shook his head. 'No. It would have been a kindness, but I couldn't do it. To kill a man, an opponent, in a fight is one thing. To kill a helpless man in cold blood another, and, for me, impossible. I make no claims to be a choir-boy—but neither am I a *guerrillero*! So I gave the monk the flask of brandy I carried, and told him to get the boy drunk—and I stumbled out of that place and was violently ill on the steps. What's the matter?' he added sharply. 'Are you faint? You asked me to tell you about it.'

Miguel, Miguel . . . The name ran through Mariana's head, together with jumbled phrases from the letter which had brought her the news of her brother's death.

'. . . discovered mortally wounded but still living on the field, by the monks of . . . taken by them to their church . . . a French officer, who happened to be there, was sufficiently moved by pity to leave some brandy . . .'

'I'm not faint,' she said. 'I'm all right.'

The time for weeping had long gone by, and the time for vengeance, that blind passion which blots out the subtle truths of human nature. She felt a strange sort of peace come over her, as if Miguel were finally laid to rest.

As night fell and a cold, clammy dew began to form on the ground, they returned to the high road, where a small and dirty-looking inn offered travellers an uninviting aspect.

'It will have to do,' Guy said. 'We've lost the Germans, anyway. Now all we'll have to contend with will be the fleas!'

The inn had few patrons, perhaps not surprising, given its condition. After they had stabled the horses they made their way to the corner of the enormous kitchen which was the only public room offered downstairs, and ordered dinner.

The hostess, a scrawny woman with dirty petticoats, proceeded to curse the cook and belabour him about the head with a ladle. This, apparently, was the usual means of communicating customers' orders to him, for eventually two plates of spiced sausage, fried in oil and swimming in grease, appeared together with a bottle of dark red, sour wine.

'In France . . .' Guy began, studying this unappetising menu, but did not complete his sentence. Perhaps words failed him.

As they ate, some more people came in, among them a young gipsy, carrying a guitar. He was a handsome fellow, lithe and supple as a cat, showily dressed in a red waistcoat and polished top-boots, with gold rings in his ears. He had thick, glossy, curly black hair, and very white teeth that gleamed against his brown skin. He smiled and bowed gallantly towards Mariana, and taking up a position near the fireplace, struck a few chords on his guitar.

'You have an admirer,' Guy remarked, grimacing as he swallowed his wine. 'You're about to be serenaded. I shall have to pay him, I suppose, for his gallantry.'

'I hope not—I'd rather not be serenaded at all,' she returned uneasily.

The gipsy's dark eyes twinkled at her knowingly, in a manner she disliked, as though something amused him. There was a bold admiration in his look which she found both offensive and disturbing. She was glad when, after a few minutes, he turned his full attention to his guitar and began to play.

'He plays well,' Guy commented. 'A musician.'

'Guy,' Mariana whispered. 'I don't want to stay in this room. I don't like that gipsy, or his music. I—I seem to have heard that tune before.'

'All these gipsy guitarists play in the same style as far as I can tell,' he said.

'Perhaps, but someone in Felipe's camp played a guitar. I never saw his face, only his outline against the firelight. But that gipsy puts me in mind of him, and I'm sure that's the tune he played!'

Guy glanced shrewdly at the gipsy. 'I don't recall him, and most of the faces of those devils are burned into my memory. Spain is full of gipsies and guitars. But if you're unhappy, we'll withdraw discreetly. We'll need to get some sleep if we're to be off early tomorrow.'

He signalled to the angular hostess, who led them up the rickety wooden staircase, passing the gipsy on the way. He murmured a flattering compliment to Mariana as she passed, the same impudent twinkle in his eyes.

The hostess flung open the door of a bedroom at the rear of the inn, announcing with pride that it was the best they had, and she herself and her late husband—God rest his soul—had spent their wedding night in it.

'And put a blight on their married life for all time, I should imagine,' Guy observed dourly when she had left. He walked across to the huge carved bedstead and dragged back the dingy sheet, holding up the one candle the hostess had left them. 'I don't advise you to get actually into this, Mariana, unless you want the company of a colony of bedbugs. Just lie down on the top and put the coverlet over you.'

'Where will you sleep?' Mariana asked in as even a tone as she could manage.

He glanced across to her, the flickering candleflame dancing mockingly across his face.

'Don't panic. I'm not going to do as I did before,' he said drily. 'My hand on my heart, I won't touch you.' His mouth twisted into a bitter grimace. 'After all, I'm no unwashed *guerrillero*. I've no ambition to follow the White Wolf in your affections, or to take his place in your bed. I'll leave the dubious comfort of our hostess's pillows to you, and sleep in the chair. Just lend me one of the blankets.' His eye lit on her mockingly. 'If you're feeling romantic, you'll have to send down for the gipsy to come up and entertain you. I'm sure he'd be willing—and talented.'

'I suppose you feel you have a right to insult me,' Mariana said quietly. 'Perhaps you have.'

He made no reply, dragging one of the woollen blankets from the bed and draping it over his shoulder, which somehow gave him the look of a Mexican horseman.

'Señorita!' he said politely, gesturing towards the bed with the candlestick.

He strolled across to the wooden settle by the

empty fireplace and threw down his blanket, before blowing out the candle.

Mariana stumbled towards the bed in the darkness and lay down unhappily on the top of it. She expected to remain awake for a while, but the cumulative exhaustion of the last three days overtook her and she fell asleep instantly, as soon as her head touched the grimy pillows.

When she awoke after a very sound sleep, her limbs were stiff and she was cold. She realised the night must almost be over, and the time near to dawn. Across the room, in the darkness, she heard the settle creak and Guy heave a sigh. He, too, was awake, and she wondered whether he was in pain.

'Guy,' she whispered, turning her head towards the sound, 'are you all right? Do your ribs hurt?'

'Not more than usual,' his voice came back across the darkened room, a touch of weary irritability in it.

'You should have had the bed,' Mariana said contritely. 'I could have slept perfectly well on the settle. Have you been awake all night?'

'Your solicitude touches my heart!' his voice said sarcastically. 'I've been awake an hour or so, not because of my ribs. I've been thinking—about how best to cross the mountains . . . and other things.'

'Will you take me with you?' Mariana asked hesitantly and held her breath.

—'Part of the way, perhaps. I'm sorry I had to bring you along on this unpleasant journey.' His voice was cold, and slightly edgy, the only sign of emotion. 'I know it's been hard for you.'

'Worse for you, Guy,' she replied. 'You are wounded, and risk capture.'

'I'm stronger than you, and used to a pretty rough life. It's made me a pretty rough person,' he added with unexpected frankness.

'You are not the only person this war has destroyed,' Mariana said with a sigh.

She heard him draw a deep breath, and then a movement, as he stood up, and the creak of his footsteps on the floorboards, coming towards her. She could sense his presence by the bed and very faintly make out his form. The side of the bed sank beneath his weight as he sat down.

'Marianne,' he said firmly, as though he had reached some decision. His fingers touched her hair, tumbled on the pillow, and her heart began to beat painfully. 'I want to say something about him . . .'

'Don't!' she interrupted. 'I don't want to talk any more about Felipe, ever.'

'Frankly, neither do I,' he admitted. 'But this is something I want to tell you while I have the opportunity, strange as it may sound to you.'

He paused, and his fingers stroked her chestnut locks briefly, before he took away his hand.

'I don't need to remind you how much I wanted to capture him. From my own point of view, there is no way I can regret his death. But you—you saw him differently. From your point of view, his loss is—is significant. I'm sorry, for your sake, that I had to kill him, and especially before your eyes. That was distressing for you.'

'I didn't love him, Guy!' Mariana caught at his hand in the darkness and felt his grip tighten momentarily on hers, before it slackened. 'I never loved him. It's true, I swear! And I was never in his bed!'

Believe me, believe me . . . she begged silently in her heart.

'He loved you!' his voice said sharply.

'No, not really! He wanted me—I was a sort of symbol. Being able to come down from the hills and marry me would have signified victory to him, don't you see? The end of all the fighting, and hiding and running.'

'And you would have married him?' His hand, in hers, was as cold and rigid as marble.

'I could not have refused him, Guy,' Mariana said miserably. 'I was his reward. That doesn't mean I wanted to marry him. I dreaded the very thought of it. It hung over me like a terrible nightmare.'

He gave a sigh, of relief as it seemed. 'Well, it's something to know I didn't kill the man you loved.'

'I couldn't love a man like that, Guy,' she protested. 'Although, perhaps, he wasn't always like that, perhaps the war made him such a terrible person. Before the war, he was my brother's friend. Miguel wasn't like that! Miguel was a gentle, kind person . . .'

And he deserved a kinder, gentler death, she thought, but that was past now. It could not be altered.

'If Felipe was ever Miguel's friend,' she went on,

'then Felipe must once have had some qualities which all that time in the hills destroyed. I'm not defending him, Guy, because I know he was a monster. But it's hard to believe Miguel could have made a friend of such a man.'

'Perhaps,' Guy said slowly, 'in your brother's company he was a better man. Just being with a good person can bring out qualities a man may never show at any other time. Just as the company of a bad one can corrupt.'

'Perhaps.' Mariana sighed. 'You must not feel badly about killing him. Someone had to do it. Like a mad dog, he had to die.'

He was silent for so long after this that she felt he expected her to continue.

'It will be over for us all soon, Guy. It will all be just a bad memory,' she said in gentle encouragment.

'Much more than that, to me,' he said abruptly. 'Far, far more!'

And for me . . . she thought miserably to herself, tossing her head restlessly on the pillow.

Make him want you, her godmother had said, with unconscious irony.

He didn't want her, not now. She had betrayed him and she would always be, in his mind, the White Wolf's woman, whether or not she had managed to convince him she had not loved Felipe. Yet he had wanted her once, a physical desire, perhaps, and no more and, as such, scorned and rejected by her. But now she wanted him so much it struck her almost as an actual pain. She ached to feel his arms around her and his mouth on hers, to reach out in the darkness and touch that bronzed muscular body lying beside her. She longed at this minute to twist her arms about his neck and draw him down on the pillows beside her, but she did not dare. He would only despise her more. She had killed the naissant flame of interest in him, even as it flickered into hesitant life. It was dead, one more casualty of a bitter war. And now that he had satisfied himself that he had not killed the man she had loved, the last vestige of any interest in what happened to her was erased from his mind. He would never come to her as a lover, she thought. She would never again feel the caressing touch of his hand on her body.

If a woman loses a man, she has no one but herself to blame.

Guy would never belong to her, but perhaps he had always, really, belonged to another.

'You must think ahead,' she urged him, a lump in her throat. 'To the future. Think about—about Lisette,' her voice faltered.

'I should like to see her again,' he said quietly, 'If Fate allows it.'

'I'm sure she's longing to see you,' Mariana forced herself to say in a small, flat voice.

'Yes. Family reunions are always emotional affairs. I expect the children are all quite grown. I shouldn't know them. They were only babies when I left.'

Mariana felt as though she had been struck by a bullet in the heart. She had never—not in her wildest moment—ever considered that he might be married. He wore no ring, but then, he could have lost that anywhere, paid a bill with it, gambled it away. A wife? Children? She jerked her hand from his.

'It—it will be—' Try as she might, she could not complete her sentence.

'I only hope,' he said, 'that my nephews don't expect their uncle to ride up covered in medals and glory!'

'Nephews!' Mariana blurted out more loudly than she intended. 'I thought you meant your children!'

'Mine?' he exclaimed in evident surprise. 'I suppose, to be honest, I'd have to admit it's not impossible, but to the best of my knowledge, I haven't got any!' He paused. 'Lisette is my sister,' he said. 'Did you think she was my wife?'

'I—I didn't know . . .' Mariana faltered, horribly embarrassed.

'That will teach you to read other people's letters!' Humour lightly touched his voice.

The bed creaked as he stood up and moved away towards the windows. In a different, more sober, tone he continued, 'It is not all over for me, Marianne. Not even the fighting. If I can find any of our units . . .'

He wrenched open the window shutters and a grey leaden light permeated the room.

'It's almost dawn,' he observed. 'Get yourself ready, and we'll go down and see if we can get ourselves some breakfast. I think I hear someone stirring below. I want to be away from here as soon as possible.'

By the time they went out into the stable yard, it was the scene of quite some activity, the ostlers shouting to one another and joking in the early morning sunshine. The door to the long, low stable stood open and Mariana followed Guy inside to where the acrid scent of horses and the sweet scent of hay were mingled on the air.

Their horses stood at the far end. A groom, crouching down with his back to them, was brushing one of them energetically.

'We are ready to leave,' Guy said to him.

The man stood up, a large, shambling and chillingly familiar figure, and turned towards them, tossing aside the body-brush.

'Welcome, Frenchman, and you too, Doña Mariana,' said José amiably, with a smile of his blackened teeth. 'I have been waiting for you.'

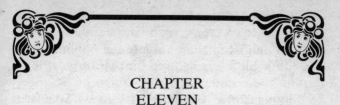

CHAPTER
ELEVEN

'How DID you find us, José?' Mariana asked wearily. A dull, heavy feeling of helpless resignation closed on her heart, and echoed in her voice.

'The gipsy sought me out last night and told me you were here. You see, señorita, I knew the Frenchman would pass this way sooner or later, so the gipsy and I, we set a watch between us. I confess, I did not expect to see you with him, Doña Mariana.'

'The lady did not come with me willingly,' Guy said strongly. 'I forced her to accompany me. I suppose you mean to kill me—but let her go free.'

José grunted and nodded. 'You are a remarkable man, Frenchman. To kill the White Wolf was quite a feat. It's pity you won't live to see your grandchildren and tell them of it! Isn't that so, Luisito?'

There was a rustle among the hay bales behind them, and the gipsy emerged, grinning, and saluted them cheerfully with a half-eaten apple he held in lieu of his guitar.

'I respect your courage, Frenchman,' José went on. 'You are a worthy enemy and I bear you no ill-will, personally. But, as an intelligent man, you will understand that I am obliged to kill you. Don Felipe relied on me, alive: he should still be able to rely on me, dead. It is a matter of honour. Your blood for his.' José crossed himself rapidly. 'God rest his soul—and yours, Frenchman.'

'Blood, blood!' Mariana cried. 'Can Spaniards think of nothing else? Where is Spanish honour in all this? The action you contemplate is murder!'

'Doña Mariana,' José said reproachfully. 'I hadn't expected to hear this from you. What of your unfortunate brother, whose blood also cries out for vengeance?'

'My brother's death has long been avenged!' Mariana insisted vehemently. 'Even Don Felipe told me so with his own lips. If you won't believe me, then believe him! Let Miguel rest in peace now. Nó more blood shall be shed in the name of my family. I forbid it!'

'There remains the question of Don Felipe himself,' José argued. 'It is a question of *his* honour, not your family's, nor my own. Still less that of the gipsy,' he added dismissively, 'for he pursues his own vengeance, for his own reasons.'

'I was not aware,' Guy said, 'that I had injured the gipsy in any way.'

'Ah, not you personally, Frenchman. His quarrel is with *all* Frenchmen, owing to a certain misfortune which befell a woman of his tribe at the hands of some French grenadiers. They never forgive an insult done to one of their own. But it is a matter of total indifference to him which French throat he cuts. He is not a patriot, only a gipsy.'

The young gipsy nodded, and sank his sharp white teeth into the apple with a crunch.

José tousled the gipsy's glossy mop of dark curls with a friendly, if heavy, hand.

'Luisito is an artist with a knife,' he informed them. 'It is an education to watch him.'

'I wish I could find that consoling,' Guy replied drily.

'*Vuestro merced* need not worry,' the gipsy said courteously. 'I shall make it quick.'

He fed the core of his apple to the nearer horse in a good-natured gesture oddly at variance with his coolly callous tone.

'He likes animals,' José explained to Mariana, seeing her eyes follow the gipsy's gesture and the bemused expression on her face. 'He would never harm one. Alas, I cannot say the same of his attitude to people—unless they are gipsies like himself, of course. I have known him capable of great barbarity. They are a cruel and savage race.'

Luisito, whose acquaintance with José seemed to be of long standing, did not object to this assessment of his people. If anything, he seemed to find it complimentary.

'Then either you or Luisito will have to kill me, too!' Mariana said forcibly. 'For if Captain Dupré had not killed Don Felipe, then I should have done so. I even had the stone in my hand to strike, but Captain Dupré killed him first—to save his own life, I might add. You didn't expect the Frenchman just to let Don Felipe kill him?'

She felt Guy's eyes on her face as she spoke.

José clicked his tongue disapprovingly. 'You place me in a difficult situation, señorita.'

'Then let me make it clearer,' she retorted. 'You owe a great deal to my family, not least your freedom to live your life as a smuggler. My father could have imprisoned you a dozen times. You owe me more than one favour.'

'True,' José admitted.

The gipsy was scratching the horse's head lazily and listening to them, merriment shining in his dark, lustrous eyes, which watched Mariana with especial attention.

'The war is nearly over,' Mariana pursued her argument with vigour and passion, vividly aware that on her words, and her words alone, hung Guy's only chance of survival. 'Afterwards, what will you do, José? Go back to smuggling? Perhaps it's time you stopped thinking about killing Frenchmen, José, and started thinking about renewing your links with them.'

'Hmn,' said José, rubbing his unshaven chin with his grimy paw. 'You have a shrewd head on young shoulders. But I've always said, men for war, and women for business.'

'And a gipsy for love,' murmured Luisito softly, so that only Mariana could hear him.

'I won't ask you how many men you, or this gipsy, or any of the White Wolf's band have killed these past four years!' Mariana continued forcefully, casting a scornful glance at Luisito. 'More than enough to balance the scales against Don Felipe's death, I know! It would not only be merciful to let Captain Dupré go, it would be sensible and prudent, and in no way dishonourable. The French are beaten. Let the British and our Spanish army drive them back across the Pyrenees. Your task is done.'

José glanced at the gipsy. 'See here, Doña Mariana, I'm a reasonable man. Much of what you say makes sense. What is the Frenchman's intention? To cross into France? He'll find it difficult.'

'Not if you take us, José,' Mariana said quickly. 'Take us over one of your smugglers' paths. You told me about them once, remember?'

'So, I'm not only to let him go, I'm to help him, too, eh?'

'My father often helped you,' she pointed out again.

'Well,' said José slowly, and Mariana hardly dared to breathe. '*I* might be persuaded . . .'

'What about him?' Mariana flung out her hand to point at the gipsy.

'That,' said José delicately, 'might well be a matter of payment. A gipsy will sell even his vengeance for money.'

'We can pay him,' Mariana promised. 'Will he agree to let us go?'

José glanced at the gipsy enquiringly.

'I agree,' Luisito said promptly. 'But I don't want the lady's money. She can pay me with a kiss.' He grinned impudently.

'No!' Guy lunged forward with unexpected belligerence, and José's ham-like fist struck his chest and knocked him back against the stable wall.

Her eyes dilated in astonishment, Mariana stared at the dragoon, struck by how pale he was, and the murderous look he directed at the gipsy. That Guy should voice opposition to the gipsy's's proposal was the last thing she had expected. It was hardly possible that he could object to seeing her in the gipsy's arms, despising her as he did for having been in Felipe's and for having betrayed him. Nor that he should wish to rashly jeopardise his one chance of escape.

But she was further disconcerted when Guy swung round towards her, two red spots staining his cheekbones beneath the bronze, and said, in French, in a tone of concentrated fury: 'I won't allow it! That boy is a murdering animal! A beast of prey! You cannot let him touch you!'

'I know what he is,' Mariana said quietly, in the same language. Hesitantly, she reached out and touched his arm. 'I—I appreciate your wishing to spare me this, but, don't you see, it's his price? He'll let us go, if I'll only let him kiss me. It—it can't be so bad. And it is my decision, Guy. It's my fault you're here at all, in this situation.'

'I don't ask you to pay such a price, Mariana,' he said in a low, hard voice.

'Last night,' she could not help reminding him in an undertone, 'you suggested I send for the gipsy!'

'It was a bad joke on my part, and you know it!' he said fiercely.

'Yes, I know you didn't mean it,' she said. 'But now, Guy, a kiss in exchange for a chance of freedom doesn't seem too high a price.'

Her voice faltered because the reality was that she dreaded the encounter. The handsome young gipsy with the engaging grin was, from all José had told them, the most cold-blooded of killers, devoid of any spark of humanity. The thought that such a creature would touch her filled her with a revulsion she knew she must not show.

Whether Luisito understood any of their conversation, she did not know, but he had been listening closely and now seemed to think the matter settled. He stepped forward and, grasping Mariana firmly, swept her towards him and almost off her feet, kissing her in a practised manner that suggested his amorous exploits vied with his vaunted prowess against the French.

'All right,' José growled, 'the lady's paid her forfeit, now let her go!' There was an uneasy note in his voice.

Luisito looked down into Mariana's face, his dark eyes gleaming, and said several sentences in a language she did not know, before he released her, with a flash of his white teeth, and stepped back.

'What did he say?' Mariana demanded of José breathlessly, her heart leaping up in alarm. 'What does he want now?'

José shrugged and looked mildly embarrassed. 'Who knows? He spoke his own heathen tongue. They are forbidden by law, as you know, to speak it in a public place, but they cling to it, all the same.'

'I don't need an interpreter to tell me his meaning!' Guy said savagely. 'If you, José, owe anything to this lady's family, you'll keep your tame knife-thrower there from putting his lecherous hands on her again, or, even if it *is* the last thing I do, I'll throttle the life out of him!'

'Patience, Frenchman!' said José warningly.

'I told the lady,' Luisito said boldly, 'that if she did not want to go with the Frenchman, she could come with me. If the Frenchman wants to fight me honourably for her, I accept. Give him a knife, José, and see if he can match me. But mind, you must agree, if I win, she's mine!' He ran the tip of his tongue across his white teeth in gleeful anticipation.

Mariana shrank back towards José, and Guy swore and lunged towards the gipsy. Luisito seemed to uncoil like the springing cat he so much resembled and leapt up onto a haybale in a swift, easy movement. As if by magic, the knife which had won him his bloodthirsty reputation appeared glittering in his right hand.

The encounter was prevented by José, who, moving with extraordinary agility for one of his size, placed his considerable bulk in front of Guy, at the same time placing a reassuring hand on Mariana's shoulder.

'Don't be a fool, Frenchman,' he muttered, 'and don't you be alarmed, señorita. Take no notice of Luisito,' he raised his voice and fixed the gipsy with a look. 'It's only his gipsy boasting. I know for a fact he has a wife already among his people, and one of whom he is mortally afraid!'

'You lie, *gorgio*!' said Luisito with a chuckle. But with a sudden characteristic change of mood, he seemed all at once to lose interest in the quarrel. He put the knife away, jumping down from the haybale and, to Mariana's inexpressible relief, turned his back on them and began to speak softly to the nearer horse in his own gipsy language, running his hand down the animal's shining neck.

'Pay him, Frenchman,' José urged in a low voice, 'and pray he accepts the money!'

Guy passed Doña Eugenia's leather wallet, which Mariana had given him, to José, who thrust it in turn into Luisito's hand. The gipsy pushed it carelessly into his pocket without opening it, and went out of the stable.

'A bad moment,' said José, wiping his brow. He stared thoughtfully at the two horses. 'These beasts will not be able to cross by the path over which I'll take you, Doña Mariana. A mule or a donkey just possibly, perhaps, but not these two horses.'

'We must try,' Guy said tersely. 'We shall need the horses on the other side.'

José shrugged. 'As you wish. But you must expect one or the other to break a leg. The path is steep and narrow. Well, we had best begin, while the sun is out—and Luisito is counting his money. The mist can come suddenly across the mountains, and a man is lucky to see a hand in front of his face.'

Luisito was perched on a fencepost in the sun, his guitar in the crook of his arm. He watched them ride out and, as Mariana passed him, the gipsy threw out one slim, steel-fingered brown hand and caught at the bridle.

'If you tire of the Frenchman,' he whispered to

her invitingly, 'have José bring you back. You wouldn't tire of me!'

Mariana jerked the reins from his grasp and rode quickly on, hearing his laughter behind her.

Slowly they rode up into the mountains. José went first, leading one horse, and Guy followed on foot, leading Mariana's horse by the bridle.

'You will have to dismount and walk soon, señorita!' José called back to her. 'If the horse goes over the edge, we don't want you going with it!'

This quickly proved no idle warning. The path grew frighteningly steep and terrifyingly narrow, winding its way across a cliff face. On the right hand it plunged down into a dizzy ravine at the bottom of which a mountain stream glittered like silver.

Mariana, following now on foot, was horrified to see the horse which José led suddenly slip and stumble. A cascade of stones clattered away down the cliff face, the horse neighed shrilly and José hauled at the bridle, cursing. Miraculously, after one hind leg had beat helplessly on the air above the ravine, the animal managed to scramble back onto the path.

'All right, Mariana?' Guy called back to her where she had stopped, flattened against the cliff face, to watch the horse's struggle.

Mariana nodded, white-faced. The silver stream, winding its way below, seemed to exercise a beckoning, hypnotic effect, calling to her.

'Don't look down!' Guy shouted at her. 'Mariana, keep your eyes on me!'

Mariana swallowed with difficulty and nodded, edging her way cautiously after the two men.

Eventually they came out onto a stony slope and José demonstrated how they must walk in a pigeon-toed fashion to prevent themselves sliding. After this came a stretch of flatter ground covered with thin grass, and here José stopped for a rest. There was no sign of any kind of beaten path, and so she presumed José took his bearings from landmarks in the circle of mountains about them. She had noticed that several times, during their traverse of the cliff, José had glanced back, not to her, but to the path behind her.

Guy had noticed it too, and now she heard him ask the smuggler in a low voice, 'Whom do you think might follow us?'

'One cannot altogether trust the gipsy,' José returned quietly. 'They owe no real loyalty to any but their own people, and although there is no one I would rather have by me in a fight than Luisito, still I know he can be fickle and capable of cutting your throat and mine for either of these two fine horses—or for the girl . . .' José glanced at Mariana. 'I'll tell you the truth, Frenchman. It was that which decided me to bring you across. You saw how he took a fancy to her, and when he's in love he's a devil. I was never so relieved as when I saw him accept the money instead of her.'

Mariana shivered and glanced behind her nervously.

Their way was easier now. She experienced that strange euphoria which comes from the clear air of the mountains. It was as if their cares were left behind, far below—even the gipsy no longer mattered—and they travelled across the roof of the world.

It was not the only thing which made her heart feel lighter and her spirits rise. An incredible idea was dancing in her mind. Was it possible, after all, that Guy did care, just a little? He had been filled with such fury at the gipsy's proposal that he must surely have felt at least some trace of personal interest in the affair. True, he hated all the *guerrilleros* with a tenacity born of what he had seen of their handiwork against the French. His loathing for Luisito had perhaps its roots in this. But, nevertheless, he had been prepared to fight the gipsy for her. A man would not do that for a woman he despised entirely, surely?

If their path was easier, the weather was deteriorating. Shreds of mist swirled about them and it had begun to rain. They and the horses slipped on the wet ground. Mariana tucked up her petticoats and made the best speed she could, not wishing to slow them all down. She could hear the noise of rushing water growing ever closer, and by the early afternoon they had reached a natural sheltered hollow in the rocks, overlooking the river whose silver course she had earlier observed so unnervingly from above. José directed them to make a fire under an overhanging ledge, and himself went to lie down on his stomach by the river bank, staring down into the water, not moving a muscle.

'What's he doing?' Mariana whispered to Guy.

'Fishing!' Guy told her briefly.

The overhanging rocks formed a shallow cave which was quite dry. Signs of previous fires on the ground indicated that this was a regular stopping-point for the smuggling fraternity. They pushed together some twigs and dry grass and struggled to strike the flint and set the tinder to smoulder. There were some pine-cones at the back of the cave. As there were no trees hereabouts, these must have been brought deliberately as a fuel store. They burned with a pungent, aromatic scent.

Guy sat back and surveyed their efforts with satisfaction. 'José will have to hurry, though,' he said, 'and catch his fish before our fire is all burned out again.' He rubbed his forehead with the heel of his palm, leaving a black smear across it. He looked tired, the signs of strain evident in the lines about his eyes and mouth.

'Guy,' Mariana whispered, almost afraid to speak. 'Why did you challenge the gipsy over me?'

Guy leaned forward and blew on the tentative flames. 'Did you want to go with him?' he asked sardonically. 'I wouldn't have interfered if I'd known. You realise he'd beat you, and probably finish by selling you to one of his gipsy brothers?'

'Would you have cared?'

Guy picked up a stick and poked it into the crackling pine-cones, watching the flames leap up. 'Someone had to defend what was left of your Spanish honour, since you seemed to have abandoned it!' he said brusquely.

'And that's all it was?' Mariana asked.

'Why, what else should it be?' He glanced up at her. 'What else would make it worth my while to fight over you?'

Mariana felt the blood rush into her face at the calculated insolence of his tone. Disappointed and humiliated, she said angrily, 'I could ask José to turn back and just abandon you here! You'd never find your way.'

'Why don't you?' His grey eyes held hers levelly.

'Don't you know?' Mariana cried out, the agony unbearable. 'Don't you really know, Guy?'

There was a splash and a shout of triumph from José, who came back grinning, with a fine trout wriggling in his hands. Broiled over their fire, it made a feast.

But José would not let them linger, and once they had eaten, they set off again. By now they were descending and the path grew erratic. At one point it was sliced into two by a narrow but deep ditch. Mariana had to slip and slide down one side of it, and scramble, grazing her hands and tearing her skirts, up the other, while Guy and José persuaded the horses to jump across.

The sun had begun to set, touching the mountain-tops with a strange glow. The going became easier and José visibly more cheerful. They were now following a rough path, little more than a sheep-track, but quite distinct. At one point they passed between two stout staves driven, for no obvious reason, into the rocky ground on either side of the track. Mariana wondered vaguely whether they had something to do with the sheep, and was puzzled as to why José reached out and patted one of the staves as he passed, giving a throaty chuckle.

Further signs of life now appeared, one or two primitive dwellings and their first fellow human being, a shepherd, accompanied by two huge savage Pyrenean dogs with long matted hair.

At long last, in the early evening, they reached the outskirts of a large settlement and halted in the steady drizzling rain which had been their companion for a while.

'Where is this place?' Mariana asked José. 'How far is it to the French border?'

'Oh, the border,' said José, with the familiar contempt of the smuggler for a thing which both earns him his living and demonstrates the ineffectiveness of governments in stopping a man going about his chosen business. 'You mean those posts back there. I thought you understood what they were. You've been on French soil this past half-hour or so!'

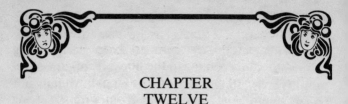

CHAPTER
TWELVE

'GUY!' MARIANA exclaimed, turning towards him, but then fell silent.

Guy was standing very still, his face expressionless, staring down at the ground. Then he stooped and touched the earth very lightly with his fingertips before straightening up and giving himself a shake, as though he had been asleep and roused himself.

Mariana went quietly to him and gently took his hand.

'You did it, Guy, you reached France. You've come home.'

He hunched his shoulders slightly. 'I'm still a long way from my home,' he said. 'But it's a beginning.'

'And nothing more, if we stay about here in the open,' José said bluntly. 'For all I know, the British could be this far already. You see that house over there?' He pointed to a long, low building. 'I used to do business with the owner before the present war. He'll be able to tell us what's happened. He's the mayor of this place.'

'The mayor—a smuggler?' Guy exclaimed.

'I did tell you,' Mariana reminded him. 'They

don't think it's a crime. It's just something everybody does.'

José signalled to them to keep back in the shadows and, crossing to the house, rapped a peculiar pattern of knocks on the door. After a few moments a voice called out from within, asking suspiciously who was there. José and the voice then engaged in a long conversation, again in a language Mariana did not know, but which Guy at least recognised.

'Basque,' he whispered in her ear.

José was beckoning to them urgently. Guy seized Mariana's hand and they ran across the cobbled street to find themselves being welcomed into the house by a small, rotund, balding man, who half pushed and half led them into a large low-raftered kitchen.

The stone floor was spotless, the furniture well scrubbed and the heat stifling. At the huge stove, a large matron with a red kerchief presided over a black cauldron of soup which she left off stirring in order to welcome her visitors and urge them to sit down.

In addition, from beside the stove, a third person rose to greet them, a shambling, shock-headed youth with the frame of a Hercules, who grinned at them diffidently and blushed deep pink when Mariana smiled back.

'My wife,' announced the diminutive mayor proudly, laying a proprietorial hand on the brawny arm of the cook, 'and my son.'

The youthful giant ducked his head.

'Ah, José,' said the mayor regretfully. 'We've not seen you in a long time. But it seems our troubles will soon be over, and we shall be back to business as usual!' He cheered up slightly, and went to fetch a bottle and some glasses from a cupboard.

José glanced cautiously at Guy and said, 'Time will tell.'

But the mayor's wife had discovered the sorry state of Mariana's clothing and, clucking her tongue in a dismayed fashion, bore her away and divested her of her damp and muddied gown.

'You are like a little sparrow!' exclaimed the good lady, observing Mariana's slight build and comparing it with her own ample contours. 'My gowns would fit you twice over. But you must wear something while yours is drying out. What shall we do? Ah, I have it!'

She threw open the lid of a large oak chest of venerable age, and began to rummage energetically inside. At last she emerged triumphant with a brocade sack-dress with a square neck and ruffled sleeves, such as had been fashionable forty years before.

'My own mother's wedding-dress! Only see what a tiny thing she was, just like you,' enthused the mayor's wife kindly. 'It's never been worn from that day till this, and has lain here all that time, waiting for a bride to wear it again. But, alas, I could not wear it at my wedding,' she added regretfully, 'for I was always plump, and my mother would not even allow me to try it on, I recall, for fear I should burst all the stitching. Look, you must step into it, like this . . .'

She helped her into the sack-dress, hooking it up with nimble fingers, and then left her in a large panelled parlour while she went to dry and repair Mariana's own gown.

There was a mirror on one wall, and Mariana went to survey her reflection in the bride's gown. For someone accustomed to the high-waisted, slim dresses of her own time, it was an odd experience to see herself in this elaborate gown with its stiffened bodice and wide skirts. She might have been looking at the ghost of her own grandmother. Mariana picked up a hairbrush which the mayor's wife had given her, and carefully brushed out her long hair, arranging it about her pale face and twisting the chestnut locks round her finger to recurl them.

It was as she was finishing this toilette that a knock at the door set her heart beating in trepidation.

'Come in!' she called in a low voice, setting down the brush and twitching at the low square neck of the gown in a last-minute adjustment.

She knew it was Guy. He entered now, bending his head beneath the low lintel, and smiled slightly when he saw her.

'You look like Cinderella,' he said.

'It's a wedding-dress—' Mariana began in explanation, spreading her hands over the full skirts. She broke off in some confusion, as his eyes met hers.

'I see,' he said.

He looked away from her and walked across to the window. Outside, it was twilight. The mountains were dark giants settling down to slumber, and the wind rattled at the wooden shutters as if to remind the householders that it was time to make them fast for the night.

'I have been talking to our host,' Guy went on soberly. 'That boy, his son, is hiding out here from conscription. It seems the countryside around here is full of deserters and runaway conscripts. At first, he tells me, the gendarmerie made regular raids and searches to flush them out. But now they no longer even bother to come, and our runaway sits openly by his mother's fireside.' He gave a snort of rueful disgust.

'You can't blame them, Guy,' Mariana said. 'They are simple people. Wars made by kings and emperors mean nothing to them.'

'And interrupts their smuggling business, I know! Well, I don't blame them. But I can't pretend that things look anything but very bad. There has been a great battle, in the East at a place called Leipzig. They have only just had news of it here.' He paused. 'It seems the Emperor was beaten and the French army retreats in total disarray.' He struck his hand impatiently against the wooden panelling round the window. 'They say the Allies have already declared for the Bourbon cause, and the Emperor may even abdicate in favour of the young King of Rome to try and head them off. But the Bourbons will not stand aside for a four-year-

old child and let the prize they have coveted so
long, and deserve so ill, slip from their grasp!'

'And you, Guy, what will you do?' Mariana
asked.

He shrugged. 'The British already control the
open passes of the Pyrenees. I shall try and find the
forces which Marshal Soult is rallying for the de-
fence of France. He will need every man—even the
half-fit, like me.'

'Fight on?' Mariana cried. 'But you've just said
it's all over, Guy! It's finished!'

'Not while I wear this uniform . . .' he said
harshly.

Mariana was silenced and sank slowly onto the
nearby sofa. The brocade skirts rustled as they
settled about her, and she automatically smoothed
them out straight, not knowing what to say or do.
Her heart ached for him, and she wished desperately there was something she could say to make him
change his mind, but knew there was nothing. His
loyalty to the oath he had sworn his Emperor was
unshakeable.

'I can tell you how it was, Marianne,' he said
slowly from the window, as if he read her thoughts.
'But I can't tell you what it was like to be a part of it.
When I was a youngster, as I told you, they set me
to study the law. It was not an inspiring choice!
There I sat, surrounded by dusty tomes, and outside the streets rang with French victories. I saw the
soldiers of the Consulate, as it then was, pass by the
windows, some of them boys no older than I was,
but to me they looked like a race of gods. I threw

away my books, I ignored my father's advice, I broke my poor mother's heart and left my sisters in tears, and went—no, ran!—to wear a uniform and ride out to conquer with all the rest and share the magic and the glory. It was a wonderful time, Marianne. The name of France was on the lips of every nation. Governments feared us and the very beggars in the streets of London and Vienna, Berlin and St Petersburg knew what France did. It was as if the keys of Europe lay at the feet of any Frenchman who cared to stoop and pick them up.'

He shrugged his shoulders and tapped a rapid rhythm on the wooden window-frame with his fingers. 'And now,' he shook his head disbelievingly, 'it's like a child watching a snow fort melt in the sun. He can't stop it, everything he's built which looked so solid and so beautiful, slipping and sliding away.'

Mariana had lived all her adult life with the name of Napoleon Bonaparte ringing in her ears. But now, as she listened to Guy, she realised for the first time, with a deeply-felt shock, the power of the spell that the man had cast over an entire generation. As Guy had said, it was the end of an epoch. Like a meteor, the French star had illuminated the sky for a brief span. Now it was all but burned out, leaving behind only bitter men and lonely women.

Mariana bowed her head. 'Perhaps he does hate me,' she thought miserably, 'for being a part of all that which destroyed French hopes, for being on the side of the victorious.'

Guy was staring moodily out into the gathering darkness. A few raindrops pattered against the panes like the rattle of a distant military drum calling to arms.

'José crosses back into Spain in the morning,' he said abruptly. 'If the weather is not too bad and there's no mist, he'll take you with him, back to your home. If the weather makes the trip too dangerous for you, you'll have to stay here. If the British come—'

He paused and, in a cold, deliberate voice, corrected himself. 'When the British come, I advise you to seek out the senior British officer and request his protection. You will be quite safe. The British are very scrupulous about that sort of thing.' He glanced at her, his mouth twisted briefly into its wry, lop-sided smile. 'It's something to do with being a gentleman. No one will try and rape you, as I did!'

'I want to go with you, Guy,' she whispered.

He drew in his breath sharply, almost as if she had again struck against his injured ribs and a spasm of pain ran through him.

'No!' he said savagely.

'You won't forgive me,' Mariana said dully.

'It's myself I don't forgive!' he burst out. 'I would forgive you anything!' He whirled round from the window and, crossing the room with a rapid step, threw himself on the sofa beside her, grasping hold of her shoulders tightly.

'Listen to me, Marianne, listen! You didn't betray me—I betrayed myself! Do you not know why?

It was because I love you, do you hear me, I love you!'

He drew a deep breath and the painful grip he had on her shoulders slackened as he gently caressed her neck. 'I have loved you and wanted you since I first set eyes on you, the night Beaudoin brought you to the house.' He slipped his arms round her and drew her towards him, burying his face in her hair. 'You were like some beautiful, wild creature,' he whispered, 'a fawn—frightened and brave, fragile and enchanting. I could have killed those men who laid their filthy hands on you! I wanted to tell you not to be afraid of me, that I wouldn't harm you—and God knows, Marianne, I wouldn't have done you any injury, even that time when I was drunk and came to your room! Crazed as I was, what with the wine, and loving you and not being able to tell you of it, and fearing you loved someone else, yet I could not have hurt you!'

Guy sighed. 'I wanted you so badly, Marianne. Yet there were times when I could not bear to see you or have you near, because I knew you couldn't be mine and I could never tell you how I felt. In the end, I did the most stupid thing of all. I deceived myself. A glance in the mirror should have been sufficient to warn me. It would have shown me the reflection of a man who was French—which you hated; a soldier—like those who killed your brother; and disfigured enough to make me repulsive not just to you, but to any woman! Yet I managed to persuade myself that one day you would let me touch you, that I would not always be an enemy. No man was ever more foolish than I, my dear, not because I trusted you foolishly, but because I allowed myself dreams to which I had no right!'

'No, Guy, no . . .' Mariana whispered, placing her fingers over his lips. 'Don't say such things, don't blame yourself . . .'

He took her hand and kissed her wrist softly. 'And, like all lovers, I was jealous, Marianne. My jealousy was a terrible thing. It burned inside me like a consuming fire. I hated *him*. Even before I knew who he was, when I thought he was just some wretched Spanish deserter, I hated him, and I feared him, because jealousy is fear, fear of losing what you most desire!'

'But I didn't love Felipe!' Mariana cried out.

'How could I be sure of that?' Guy insisted. 'Why shouldn't you have loved him? You took risks for him no woman takes for a man who is nothing to her! He was always there. Alive, and even more so when he was dead, he stood at my shoulder all the time! In the camp, all the time I was in their hands, the only image which haunted my brain was one of you in his arms! It was the worst of all. Nothing they did to me could cause me as much pain and wretchedness as the thought that you were with him.

'I tried to hate you then, Marianne, to protect myself. I tried to do it, and I couldn't. Afterwards, I tried to pretend I no longer cared, but I did care! The night I forced you to escape with me and we rested in the shepherd's hut, I watched you sleeping and I kissed you before you woke, and knew that I was doomed to always love you . . . and I could never let you belong to any other. I thought you saw it yourself this morning, when that murdering gipsy defiled you with his touch, and I could not keep silent—'

'And they hurt you so,' Mariana said miserably, smoothing his hair, 'I hurt you so . . .'

'Not you,' he contradicted her obstinately. 'I was the one who wanted to capture the White Wolf so much I let my wish cloud my judgment, and I was the one who refused to believe you could be the White Wolf's woman—'

'I wasn't his woman!' Mariana protested. 'Only in his mind, never in mine, except as a kind of fate I would have done almost anything to escape. Surely you don't still think I loved him, not after all that's happened?'

'No. I feared it until last night, at the inn.' He gave a mirthless little laugh. 'I should have been happy to hear you say you'd never loved him. In fact, it made me more wretched, because I knew then that I could never ask you to love me.'

'You told me once, Guy,' Mariana reminded him gently, 'that the time would come when you wouldn't have to ask. Do you remember?'

'I remember,' he said, and his voice shook slightly. 'I've said a lot of things to you, Marianne, which I would have done better to keep to myself.'

'That time has come, Guy,' she said. She slid her arms about his neck. 'I want to be yours, if—if you still want me.'

'You know I still want you!' he said wretchedly.

'But don't you see? The Emperor, everything, is finished. We shall fight on, but destiny has taken sides against us. I shall have nothing. No army career—the Bourbons will have no use for Napoleonic officers like me. No fortune, no future—except to go back to practising the law which I've nearly forgotten. I don't even have a whole face, only the mangled remains of one. I've nothing to offer you, Marianne, nothing to offer a wife—'

'I love you, Guy,' Mariana answered. 'It doesn't matter about the rest. We don't know what will happen now in France, but wherever you go, and whatever you do, I want to be there. I want us to be together.'

In the darkness of the mayor's parlour he leaned towards her. In his arms, she slid so easily and gently down on to the cushions of the sofa, lifting her face towards his, seeking his lips, and sensing a wild exhilaration throbbing in her at the fiercely increasing pressure of his mouth on hers.

'I don't think I could let you go,' he murmured. His voice trembled, and the touch of his fingers was damp with perspiration as his hand ran down her throat and rested on the low neck of the bride's gown. She could feel her own heart beating against his palm. He bent his head and kissed the soft swell of her breast. 'You were my prisoner,' he whispered, 'and you made me yours—for ever.'

The door creaked and the mayor, bearing a candlestick, half-entered, before exclaiming, '*Ah, pardon . . .*' as the flame of his candle fell across the couple embracing on the sofa.

'No, *monsieur le maire*, wait!' Guy jumped up as the little man began to retreat. 'There is something you can do, if you will.'

'I am at your disposal, Captain,' the little mayor said courteously, setting his candlestick down and looking at Guy enquiringly.

'In your official capacity,' Guy said, 'could you marry us? Now, if possible.'

'I should be honoured!' the mayor exclaimed. He beamed at them and clapped his podgy hands together. 'It shall be done properly! Only give me time to look out my sash of office. My wife will put it away where I can't find it. And to unfurl the flag! There shall be military honours! Ah—' he frowned, a little perplexed. 'It is the flag of the Empire. You don't object? I suppose, now, if what they say is true, we shall have to get ourselves a Royalist flag again. The old one was burned in 'eighty-nine. But, in the meantime, the flag of Napoleon is all we have.'

'I have fought beneath that flag since I was nineteen years of age,' Guy said quietly. 'I may yet die beneath it. I shall certainly be married beneath it now.'

'Then I shall go and get everything ready,' the mayor said happily.

He scuttled away and could be heard loudly declaring the news to his wife, who greeted it with shrieks of pleasure.

Guy turned to Mariana and held out his hand to her.

'A strange wedding party,' he said. 'You will be

attended by our ample hostess, and I, I suppose, by José!'

Mariana smiled at him and reached out to take his hand.

'José brought me down the hillside the night Beaudoin captured me,' she said. 'He brought me down to you.'

'Well, then,' Guy replied, as his strong fingers closed on hers. 'Let us finish what José began.'

Mills & Boon

Your chance to step into the past Take 2 Books FREE

Discover a world long vanished. An age of chivalry and intrigue, powerful desires and exotic locations. Read about true love found by soldiers and states-men, princesses and serving girls. All written as only Mills & Boon's top-selling authors know how. Become a regular reader of Mills & Boon Masquerade Historical Romances and enjoy 4 superb, new titles every two months, plus a whole range of special benefits: your very own personal membership card entitles you to a regular free newsletter packed with recipes, competitions, exclusive book offers plus other bargain offers and big cash savings.

AND an Introductory FREE GIFT for YOU. Turn over the page for details.

**Fill in and send this coupon back today
and we will send you**

2 Introductory
Historical Romances
FREE

At the same time we will reserve a subscription to
Mills & Boon Masquerade Historical Romances for
you. Every two months you will receive Four new,
superb titles delivered direct to your door. You
don't pay extra for delivery. Postage and packing is
always completely free. There is no obligation or
commitment – you only receive books for as long as
you want to.

**Just fill in and post the coupon today to MILLS & BOON
READER SERVICE, FREEPOST, P.O. BOX 236, CROYDON,
SURREY CR9 9EL.**

**Please Note:- READERS IN SOUTH AFRICA write to
Mills & Boon, Postbag X3010,
Randburg 2125, S. Africa.**

- -

FREE BOOKS CERTIFICATE

**To: Mills & Boon Reader Service, FREEPOST, P.O. Box 236,
Croydon, Surrey CR9 9EL.**

Please send me, free and without obligation, two Masquerade Historical Romances, and
reserve a Reader Service Subscription for me. If I decide to subscribe I shall receive,
following my free parcel of books, four new Masquerade Historical Romances every two
months for £5.00, post and packing free. If I decide not to subscribe, I shall write to you
within 10 days. The free books are mine to keep in any case. I understand that I may cancel
my subscription at any time simply by writing to you. I am over 18 years of age.

Please write in BLOCK CAPITALS.

Signature _____

Name _____

Address _____

_____ Post code _____

SEND NO MONEY — TAKE NO RISKS.

Please don't forget to include your Postcode.

*Remember, postcodes speed delivery. Offer applies in UK only and is not valid
to present subscribers. Mills & Boon reserve the right to exercise discretion in
granting membership. If price changes are necessary you will be notified.*

4M *Offer expires July 31st 1984.*

EP9M